Preacher Jack

and

The Fangslinger

The Fangslinger II

BRET LEE HART

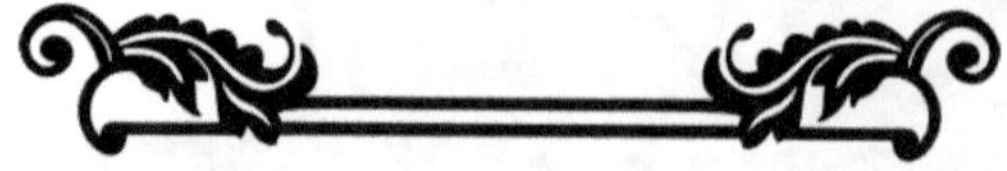

Preacher Jack and the Fangslinger
    The Fangslinger II

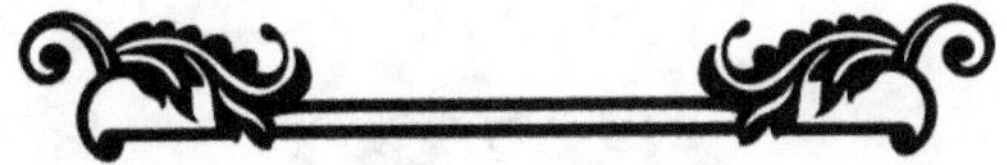

PREACHER JACK AND THE FANGSLINGER
The Fangslinger II

1 The Revelation
The Revelation of Jesus Christ, which god gave him to show his servants what must soon take place, he made it known by sending his angel to his servant John.

Who testifies to everything he saw- that is, the word of God and the testimony of Jesus Christ.

Blessed is the one who reads the words of this prophecy, and blessed are those who hear it and take to heart what is written in it, because the time is near.

PROLOGUE

The storm subsided and the earth calmed as the great White Owl flew north from the top of the Black Mesa Mountain with its talons clutching the severed head of the master vampire named Andelko Balas. The vampire's body had turned to dust, but the evil that was Andelko lived on—in the crown. The un-dead harbored no heart nor soul, only wicked power. The evil that Andelko held lived on, growing stronger within his head and behind his constant glowing red eyes. Satan's power was resilient and relentless, and he would not give up on the prize easily. Yes, the Devil knew that one day he would rule the earth by ruling the unbelievers that lived upon it as it was written in the book of Revelation, but it was not in the fallen one's nature to be patient and he refused to sit back idly and wait for that day to come.

The great White Owl flew—on across the desert as the jaw of the vampire chomped continuously at the air with his pointed fangs. The owl's talons were sunk into the cold dead flesh of the skull of the master vampire that allowed a connection between the good and the evil. The fallen one attacked, sending his darkness flowing through the head like a cancer and into the claws of the White Owl in an attempt to cause the great bird to release the skull of Andelko Balas; but the owl held strong for a time as its screeches could be heard for miles. The cancerous blackness spread and eventually covered the great bird in a wave and forced the owl to reveal its true form; suddenly, from the bottom up the solid white, naked shape of a man began to materialize. The angel wore a crown of gold and had the wings of a Pegasus. The owl had turned, forced into his original form as an angel of God, and his talons had turned into the feet of a man, not allowing him to hold on to the vampire's head any longer. Andelko Balas's detached crown fell from the sky and descended to the earth as the angel ascended up and into the heavens unwillingly. The angel was sad, for he knew he had failed and planted the seed across the land for a second battle of the flesh between the Good and the Evil.

CHAPTER ONE

Psalm 30:2
*O Lord my God, I cried unto thee,
and thou hast healed me.*

Preacher Jack Denton Anderson and Colonel Richard Andersson had left the Black Mesa Mountain behind them, traveling by wagon. The vampires from across the sea had been defeated and Jack and Richard had survived. Jack was a preacher and a gunfighter trained in the civil war and ordained by God, Richard was a Romanian soldier from another time, kept alive for many years past his due by the injections of the evil blood of the vampire, only his destiny had brought him to the good side.

The two men had traveled for six days across the Arizona desert with Colonel Richard clinging to life. The master vampire's blood that was flowing inside the soldier of Romanian descent had kept him alive for hundreds of years, but now it was infecting his body and inducing a comatose state; his heart continued to beat but his breath was weak. Jack called Richard brother and prayed for him daily.

On the seventh day of travel Jack woke an hour before the sun; his first move was to check on Richards's condition. He walked around the diminishing fire and kneeled down by his side; he put two fingers against Richards's neck feeling for a pulse. There was no change, the beats were weak and far apart, Jack closed his eyes and whispered his prayer,

"I sought the Lord, and he heard me, and delivered me from all my fears.

They looked unto him, and were lightened; and their faces were not ashamed.

This poor man cried, and the Lord heard him, and saved him out of all his troubles.

The angel of the Lord encampeth round about them that fear him, and delivereth them."

When Jack finished his prayer a wind blew, forcing his eyes open to see Richard staring back at him.

Water mouthed Richard, but no sound could be heard.

Jack quickly went for his canteen that hung from the back of his horse; as an afterthought he also grabbed a sliver of beef jerky from his saddle bag. He returned to his patient and poured water into his own open palm as he went to one knee and then slowly dripped it into Richards's mouth off the tips of his fingers. Richards parched lips burned as the cold liquid passed over them and funneled the water into his dry throat. *It is truly a miracle that this man is still alive after six plus days without food or water,* Jack thought with blessing.

Jack continued with the drips of water until Richard reached for the canteen and began to pour it down his gullet; Jack had to pull the container from his grasp.

"Easy Colonel, too much too fast will put a hurtin' on yah. Here try this."

Jack broke off a small piece of the beef jerky and placed it in his mouth; he continued on one small piece at a time until the meat was gone. He did this like a mamma bird feeding her baby, allowing Richard to have little amounts of water in-between. The Colonel fell back into a deep sleep; Jack again checked his pulse, and to his pleasure the beats were stronger and more regular. A howl could suddenly be heard off in the distance; the preacher instinctively put his hand on the butt of his holstered revolver while he stood and looked into the darkness and in the direction of the wail. A second howl came; this time it was miles closer. Jack pulled his forty-five Colt and cocked the hammer back with his thumb. Hearing a coyote sounding off in the desert was usual in these parts, but the sound he heard this morning was not a coyote but the howl of the wolf. Suddenly, the first ray of the morning sun broke across the sand with a flash that forced Jack to spin and level his revolver, preparing to shoot; there was nothing there but the blinding sun light.

"Easy simmer Jack, don't lose it now." He said aloud to himself while placing his hand on the white preacher's collar that he wore around his neck; he glanced back at Richard, only to see him resting. The sun was showing signs of a hot day beaming over the horizon; Jack holstered his weapon and took this time to walk the short distance to the river where he would relieve himself and wash up for the day. The water was cool and refreshing as he tried to rinse away the grime that had dried on his face. Jack tried to recall details of their victory against the evil on the mountain but his memories were vague at best. He suddenly saw a reflection of the master vampire's face flash off the water which gave him an eerie feeling up his spine. He stood quickly. *"Easy simmer Jack,"* ran across his mind once again.

On his return to camp, Jack was surprised to see that Richard had pulled himself up and was now leaning against a flat rock formation alongside the campsite that partially blocked the dry desert wind. As Jack got closer he could see that the color in Richard's face was much better. Jack then realized that the colonel had positioned himself in a shady spot to avoid the rays of the morning light. This concerned the Preacher, for this was something a man with the blood of a vampire might do.

"Does the sun bother you?" Jack asked.

"Slightly, yes," answered Richard, "may I bother you for some additional water?"

Jack fetched the canteen and went to one knee as he handed it over, but this time Jack did so at a greater distance.

Richard took several small sips, and then the two men stared at one another for a moment.

"You do not trust me so?"

"Ain't sure just yet," answered Jack, "you did save my life on that mountain, and the rumor is that we are kin, but the simple fact that you're hidin' from the sun does got me wonderin'."

"I am very weak," said Richard, "the vampire blood that runs through my veins that had once sustained me is now killing me."

"What can we do?" asked Jack.

"Bloodletting, have you heard of this?"

"I git what you're sayin', you sure you want to go through that? It's a slow course."

"If I do not I will die." Richard said plainly.

Jack stood and stared at this man for a moment; staring back at him was a soldier from another time and another place. Jack tried to understand who exactly this man was.

"I'm gonna need some more wood for the fire," said Jack as he turned on his heel and left to begin his search for timber. Firewood was far and in-between at times in the desert but with the river close by there was foliage about; he returned to Richard with his arms full within an hour. He dumped the whole load on the remaining hot coals and went to the wagon were he pulled the Colonel's sword from its scabbard and then returned. Jack used the blade to stoke the fire that came to life with each poke; the extra warmth caused a drip of sweat to run down Jack's face. He then placed the end of the sword among the hot coals and left it there to heat. He kneeled by Richards's side and pulled his knife from his belt; he then took the man's hand into his and bent the wrist upward.

Richard opened his eyes. While looking at the preacher he said.

"A pint will be sufficient, any more than that and I may not wake."

"I wish I had whiskey for cleaning, among other things." commented Jack.

"Do not touch the blood, Preacher for it still holds much evil power," the Colonel warned.

With a nod of understanding Jack took his blade and cut across Richard's veins at the wrist; the smell of sulfur immediately filled the air as the black cold blood seeped from Richard's body, it was very thick and took some time to drip; when the drops finally hit the ground it seemed to consume the earth. Suddenly a very large scorpion appeared from under the sand as a bead of the dark blood landed on its back; the creature raised its pincers and began to open and close them with great speed, creating a loud clacking sound, with its stinger raised in an attack position it came at Jack in a dead run; Jack quickly thrust his knife into the back of the scorpion just before it reached his knee. He turned the blade upright and brought the insect belly-up and to his level of sight, Jack could see that the eyes glowed red. The bug suddenly let out a hiss that sent a chill up Jack's back side; with disgust Jack thrust the tip of his knife into the fire, burning the scorpion up with a flash.

"What the Hell!" exclaimed Jack as he got to his feet and took a step back. A cough escaped Richard's lips, diverting Jack's attention back to his task. He grabbed the sword from the fire and took Richard's hand into his, then slapped the red hot steel to his wrist cauterizing the wound and stopping the flow of blood; Richard let out a yell and then passed out with a groan.

The bloodletting went on every three days for twelve days; as the bad blood was drained, Richards's body would make new blood to replace it, and as a result of this procedure he became stronger and more human with every letting. The blood from Richard's body was redder than it was black now and not as thick; it no longer created a mist during the letting for its temperature was warming. Richard slept in-between the drainings of his lifeblood, drinking little and eating even less. Jack continued to pray daily for Richard, and he wondered if his faith was strong enough to heal this man; this went on until the late evening of the twelfth day.

The preacher was sleeping deep and dreaming of the great White Owl flying across the sky with a severed head clutched in its talons. *Jack was following the bird from behind as if he were in flight, he could not see the face of the head but he suspected who it might belong too and a satisfying grin appeared on his face; he began to overtake the owl as he floated by its side, the great bird screeched at him with a warning call, but Jack could not slow and would soon be able to look into the eyes of the defeated master vampire Andelko Balas. Suddenly from behind and above he heard a familiar voice,*

"Do not look upon the head, Preacher, for you may not like what you see."

Fear crept into Jacks soul as he floated around to the front of the severed head, the owl screeched another warning but Jack could not control his movement. He tried to look away but he could not, the hair on the severed head began to change and to his horror he saw his own face, for the head in the owl's talons was his own. Jack let out a scream that broke the spell of his nightmare; he jumped up out of his bedroll and scrambled to his feet; his hands hovering over his pistols. It was night and the fire was burning. Sweat beaded up on his forehead.

"A nightmare?" said a voice.

Jack spun and pulled one Colt forty-five with the speed of a gunfighter.

"Calm Preacher, did you not spend weeks making repair of me, just to slay me now?"

"What the Hell, Colonel!" exclaimed Jack, as he then lowered his weapon.

"Call me Richard; I am not a Colonel any longer."

"Once a soldier always a soldier, it's in the blood." Jack replied.

"It is in the blood? The meaning by your logic, would pronounce me once a vampire always a vampire."

Jack pulled a rolled smoke from his pocket and struck a match from the back of his leg.

"The same rules don't apply when it comes to angels and demons." Jack said as if there could be no more debate. "I see you're feelin' better."

"I will live, but I ask the question why?" Richard looked to the preacher for an answer.

"I'll make some coffee," Said Jack. "We need to sit and talk for a bit, I fear our work has just begun."

Jack fetched the last of the coffee and the last of the beef jerky from his saddle bag; he was not surprised that their food lasted just long enough for Richard to heal. *The Lord will provide,* went through the preacher's mind as the two men now sat across from each other; the sun was two hours from rising and the fire was burning bright now as Richard leaned forward to drop the last of their wood onto the hot coals.

"Your boss ain't quite dead yet, somehow?" Jack said, as he sipped his coffee waiting for the Colonel to reply.

"I witnessed Andelko's head separate from his body by one swing of your silver sword in a flash of blue light, Preacher, and then I witnessed a giant white bird fly away with his head, was this not so?"

"Yep, it did happen that away, but I fear his evil still lives."

Jack let this sink in for a moment. When the Colonel did not reply Jack continued.

"Since the beginning of my reckonin' I had dreams of what was to come and then they just quit on me. Last night they started up again, for the first time since that day on the top of the mountain."

"And what did your dream speak to you?" asked Colonel Richard.

"The best I can tell is this ain't over, the good news is we might git some help."

"You speak of thy God?"

"The one and only God," replied Jack with conviction, "I believe you were spared to help me, I would even go so far as sayin' your whole life since your birth has been for this reason."

"You know what I consider?" said Richard to Jack, "I consider that we are pawns in the middle of a game that is being played by powers between up above and down below."

"I might agree with that if I git your meanin', 'cause you talk sorta funny."

Richard laughed at this, "I speak in a strange manner?"

Jack could not help himself, they both grinned at one another for a moment. Afterwards Jack continued the conversation while pouring them a fresh cup of coffee.

"You're a much better talker than my last partner was."

"Who might that have been?" asked Richard.

"Chief White Owl," replied Jack, "he saved my life from a path of ruin, but his talk was thin."

"I believe I witnessed the man you speak of, the American Indian with the feathers of a bird on top of his head in the ravine where we battled. You swung a sword of silver with a blue light; may I see it?"

Jack set down his cup and left Richard by the fire; he returned with the silver blade and pulled it from its sheath. it shined in the reflection of the fire light.

Richard stood, not taking his eyes from the sword. "Magnificent," he said, "may I hold it?"

"No one can touch it but me," said Jack. He was a little embarrassed after he realized that he had said this with some pride.

"I must," pleaded the Colonel as he reached out his hand.

Jack flipped the blade around and stretched it across the fire, hilt first; Richard reached out and grasped the handle. His facial expression changed as the sword burned into his skin. He quickly released his grip with a groan as smoke was released upward from his hand and the smell of burnt flesh filled the air.

"I warned yah," Jack said, as he then pulled the sword back and slid it into the scabbard and placed it by his side; he vowed never again would he separate himself from it until his death.

Preacher Jack and Colonel Richard talked until sunrise, telling some stories of their youth. Jack's story was much shorter than Richard's, for Richard had lived for over centuries, kept alive by injections of vampire blood. Now that they had drained most of the evil liquid from Richard's veins he had appeared to have aged somewhat, but the Colonel somehow knew he was given new life to fight the wicked that would try once again to claim the earth for its kingdom.

The Preacher was now fully grounded in his faith; he told of the flaming sword that once guarded the entrance of the Garden of Eden given to him by the Holy Spirit through Chief White Owl, for whose return Jack now longed.

In the early morning they left the camp that had been their home for weeks and headed north, not sure where Jack's dreams would lead them. The two men knew they were related somehow, they were long lost brothers reunited. This time and this place was their destiny.

Their supplies were depleted and hunting would be the priority of the day. The empty wagon was left behind as Richard rode his giant black Clydesdale from his homeland and Jack rode his black Stallion as they set out on their journey to find the master vampire's severed head.

CHAPTER TWO

Revelation 22:6
*The angel said to me, "These words are trustworthy
and true. The Lord, the God of the spirits of the
prophets, set his angel to show his servants
the things that soon must take place.*

Preacher Jack and Colonel Richard had secured
nourishment for their travels just hours after their
departure from the camp; a mule deer had crossed
their path in the afternoon of the first day. Jack placed
two silver bullets high in the neck of the animal,
putting it down quickly. They ate the liver, kidneys,
heart and tongue for supper as these organs would
spoil rapidly, and they salted the muscle meat for
future meals. Jerky was not an option, for they did not
feel they had the time for the drying. Jack's dreams
told him that time was short, and to stay on a heading
to the north until they came upon a place where the
land had been swallowed up by the earth. Jack knew
that the head of Andelko was their destination and he
sensed that his old friend Chief White Owl was guiding
him somehow.

Another day had passed and the night had settled
in, revealing a blue moon. Jack and Richard were
smoking tobacco by the fire when the wolf began to
howl.

"They have been following us," said Richard, "you know this?"

"Yep," replied Jack, "they stay out of sight but I feel them lurking just off in the distance, I can't say if they are friends or enemies."

"I cannot clarify it but the wolves somehow followed me from across the sea and from my homeland. They are all black as the night, except for their leader who is solid white and larger than the rest."

"Solid white and larger than the rest?" said Jack aloud to himself as much as to Richard, "Like the great White Owl."

"Yes," said Richard, "there appears to be a connection there, I do know that the wolves do not fear the vampires, in fact I witnessed them attack the undead in what I would call a battle victory for the pack."

"We can't forgit, brother, that the evil one is a master of deception." As the preacher said this, another howl could be heard; this one was closer than the last.

"I will take first watch," said the Colonel as he got to his feet and headed for the perimeter of the small camp. This would be the last speak of the night. Jack laid back and drifted into sleep; after a short while he began to dream. The Colonel would stay at the guard and allow the preacher to slumber until the morning, for they both knew that the dreams were guiding their direction to their next destination.

The angel Gabriel could not continue on in the form of the great White Owl, for the black evil invaded his being. The shield of good protected Gabriel from any access to his soul but it could not safeguard against the weakening of his power to maintain his method. The head of the master vampire descended to the earth from high up and then continued on past the elevation of the desert and down into the great canyon until it came to rest with a splash into the river. The severed head rushed down stream rolling just below the water line, popping up occasionally until it finally came to rest face down on the river's shore...

The Colonel turned toward the sleeping preacher from his watch as he heard him moan in his sleep; Richard went back to his guard as Jack quieted. It was now early morning, but the clouds were keeping the light from breaking through.

The little Apache girl left small moccasin foot prints on the bank as she fished along the shore of the river. She was not far from where the teepees of her Indian village of the Apache stood thirty five in all; the tribe was over two hundred strong with one hundred warriors. The six-year-old Indian child with the long jet-black hair poked at the water with a stick, practicing to fish like her sister had taught her. She looked to her right and spotted the head that was covered with muddy clumps of hair which she attempted to roll over with her stick...

"Stay away! Stay away!" came a warning from the preacher as he yelled out in his sleep, sending the Colonel to his alert.

After the second attempt the little Indian girl managed to roll the head and stood it upright onto the base of the neck; Andelko Balas's severed head spun to face her, the eyes glowed red, putting the girl into a trance; she bent down and picked up the crown of evil that began to hiss with fangs bared as she brought the head in close for a kiss...

"Nooooo...!" screamed Jack, as he scrambled to his feet; sweat covered his brow and he was breathing heavy. Richard faced him from across the fire with his sword drawn. Not just one wolf, but all the wolves were howling off in the distance, sending chills up the spines of both men.

"What in Hades do you see, preacher?" asked the Colonel.

"Your once Lord and Master Andelko Balas, I fear, has begun infecting a new coven. My dreams have shown me this."

The wolves howled once again, communicating with one another as if to warn all of the impending evil that was coming across the land. A cold wind began to blow as a morning storm formed in the sky. Jack and Richard struck camp and mounted their horses, setting out to the north for a great canyon as a steady rain began to fall.

"How far now, preacher?" asked Richard, speaking loud over the sound of the rain shower from the back of his great Clydesdale.

"I ain't sure, Colonel, but by the end of this day we will know more. We need to follow this storm to the canyon; I do believe the weather was sent to help conceal our arrival somehow."

It was too dangerous to ride hard in the storm, the desert sand had turned to mud and their visibility was minimal. The two warriors of good traveled at a walk, side-by-side looking for a sign as the rain fell harder.

Somewhere to the north the little Indian girl made her way back into the Apache village with a gift for her father cradled in her arms. A storm was moving in from the south at her back and the clouds were concealing the sun. She had awakened in the early morning from a dream that told her to go to the river, and as she returned she found that the Apache tribe still slept. She entered her father's *wickiup*; he was the chief of his people. Her mother lay beside him, also sleeping deeply. The Indian girl, now pale with eyes that glowed red and fangs that protruded from her gums, set down Andelko's crown and picked up a tomahawk, bringing it down violently on her father's neck and removing his head with a single blow. The mother sat up from her sleep with an expression of horror. She almost did not recognize her daughter as the little girl left her feet and lunged; she bit into her mother's neck, pulling on the jugular vein and ripping out her throat. She drank her mother's blood, as was now her nature; she only stopped as she was commanded telepathically by the crown of Andelko. The Indian girl left her dead mother where she lay in a pool of spilt blood and went to the vampire's head; she picked it up and brought it to her father's body and placed it onto his headless shoulders; a red flash of light lit up the walls of the *wickiup* as Andelko's head merged and became one with the Apache chief's once dead body. Andelko rose to his feet and clutched his fists, enjoying the strength of his new form; he then went to his young apostle of the un-dead and held the child vampire and brought her in close for a hug; he stroked her hair with loving affection for a moment and then twisted her neck, killing her instantly. Andelko fed upon the child and what was left of the mother's blood before he went from dwelling to dwelling and turned the male warriors who remained in his trance, up to one hundred, into a coven of Apache warrior vampires. As the braves were turned they fed upon their families as they slept, until there was not a female or child or old person left alive.

The storm had passed on to the north by the afternoon and visibility returned. The land had started out flat but for the last ten miles the terrain had begun to climb upward; as the storm moved on, Jack and Richard could see cliff formations standing in their way. They traveled another mile and with every step the rock face grew larger and blocked their path. Jack stopped his stallion and Richard did the same as they surveyed the landscape.

"What is the best course of action currently, Preacher?" asked Richard. "There appears to be a rock wall blocking our path to the north, we may have to change our direction."

"No, we need to stick to the north," Jack answered without doubt.

"We could go around the cliffs, but it would take several days to the east or to the west to continue north."

"There's no time for that," said Jack.

They sat there on top of their mounts for a moment and considered their dilemma; then Jack spotted something straight away and up high. The preacher leveled his arm out and pointed his finger toward a spot at the top of the cliff.

"Look there," he said, "a shape perched and carved in stone."

Richard followed with his eyes to where he was pointing.

"It is a marker," the Colonel said. He focused with heavy concentration, his eyes glowed red for a split second unknown to either man, and then they turned back to normal. "It is an owl carved from the rock. Can you see what it is from this distance, Preacher?"

"My sight is not as good as yours but through my faith I can see clearly."

Richard looked upon the preacher with wonder, and then he said.

"I am cursed from the remaining vampire blood that still runs through my veins, and I fear your God could not forgive the atrocities I have committed in this long life for thy enemy."

"O thou of little faith, wherefore didst thou doubt?" quoted Jack.

"You speak in tongues, Preacher, but you are correct, I have never known this faith you speak of, I have only known evil."

"God has spared you from the eternal fire, Colonel, is that not proof of forgiveness?"

"Yes, possibly. More likely I was spared for his own purpose," Richard answered reluctantly. "When the evil that is Andelko is defeated we will talk of this again, Preacher."

"I will pray for you, brother," said Jack, "Now let's git on the move, time is a wastin'."

They continued on their northern heading using the rock formation as their marker. The shape of the owl became clearer the closer they got to the rock face. They stopped thirty feet in front of the rock wall under the crude carving; it was clearly an owl carved in sand stone. Jack had a good idea who had left it for them to follow, but he was afraid to speak it out loud for he feared that by saying so would make it untrue. The men took this time to drink water from their canteens.

"What is our next move, Preacher?" Richard asked.

Jack swung down from his mount and walked over to the wall; he began sliding his gloved hand along the surface by moving from left to right and feeling for an opening. The Colonel was watching him with some interest, he looked to the east and then to the west searching for intruders, and then he turned his head and twisted his body to look behind them in the direction of the south. When Richard turned back around the preacher was gone. He pulled his sword and with one swift motion he swung his leg over the neck of his great horse and slid to the ground; he charged the sandstone wall, glancing up at the owl only once. When he reached five feet from the mountain wall, Jack suddenly appeared to Richard's left, side stepping into his view from a crevasse.

The preacher's hand went to his revolver as he stared down the point of the Colonel's blade; three seconds went by, then Richard lowered his weapon and Jack removed his hand from the butt of his pistol.

"The passageway is narrow but your steed will just fit," said Jack. "They won't like it much, but if we blindfold them I reckon we can walk them through."

"Through to where?" asked the Colonel.

"I think I know, but there is only one way to find out for sure."

They covered the horses' eyes with tied cloth and led them on foot into the rock split. Jack went first with his stallion and Richard followed at a distance as not to get kicked if the stallion began to buck. They did not have to travel far through the narrow passage before the crevasse turned back to the north and opened up wider; when Jack cleared the wall of stone he was struck with awe. He continued far enough for John to clear the crevasse and come alongside him into the opening. The Big Canyon was a sight to see before them. Jack had heard about what was known as The Jewel of Arizona, but to see it was something else. Richard Andersson's mouth dropped, for he had not even heard of such wonders.

The Grand Canyon was hundreds of miles long, tens of miles wide and over a mile deep with a moving river zig-zagging down through the middle of the enormous gorge. The afternoon sun still shined upon their face but there were pockets of rain storms to be seen across the far away sky. There were lightning bolts breaking through the black clouds; Jack thought he noticed that some of the bolts shined an unusual blue.

"This land called America continues to amaze me, Preacher."

"Our founders called it God's country," Jack replied.

"I am beginning to understand," said Richard. "I am also beginning to understand that, like the Black Mesa Mountain, this canyon will be the place of the second battle of good versus evil."

"I reckon you would be right," Jack replied in a definite tone.

They removed the cloth that had covered the eyes of their horses and then mounted up to continue north. Slowly downward they traveled wherever their animals could gain their footing. The sun would be down soon and they must find a suitable place to set up camp for the night. After a while Jack found a ledge that leveled out next to a spring that pooled up and then trickled down the rock face and created a small creek.

"This will have to do," Jack announced as he dismounted his stallion. Richard did the same as the sun was disappearing quickly behind the outer walls of the canyon to the west.

"I would expect the sun to set inside these canyon walls as vast as is the valley," Richard said with wonder. "If you will take care of the unsaddling of the horses, I will search for wood for the fire."

Jack nodded in agreement and set to work removing the horses' saddles and gear from their backs. He removed the stallion's saddle with ease, the Clydesdale's rig was different and took Jack a moment to figure out the buckles. He had to reach high to remove the saddle, being reminded how big this horse really was up so close and personal. He led the animals to the pool of water were they drank side by side; the sun was setting at one end of the canyon and being replaced by the moon at the other end. Jack was thankful that the moonlight was bright, for he could see extremely well as his eyes adjusted. A thought ran through Jack's mind, as he brushed down the animal's sweaty fur. *"How much better can Richard see in the night than I? How much of the vampire's blood still remains in his veins?"* He split up the strokes evenly between the two horses but took longer in the end with the Clydesdale from its sheer size. There wasn't as much as one blade of grass on this cliff ledge for the horses to eat, forcing Jack to use the last of his packed grain. He went to his saddle and pulled out a folded up feed bag and the remaining grain and went to the pool were the horses had begun to slow down on their intake of water. Jack held the empty feed bag up to the Clydesdale's head. Richard returned with an arm full of wood.

"This here feed bag will not fit over your horse's big snout." Jack said.

"You work the fire and I will forage him by my hand," Richard answered with some pride to his voice.

"You mean feed him, right?"

"Yes," answered Richard. "Forage is feed."

"Well why the heck didn't you just say so?" muttered Jack as he strapped the feedbag to his stallion and then walked away and over to the stack of wood. He arranged the small branches in the shape of a teepee and struck a match lighting a ball of desert moss and then wedged it under the kindling to start the fire.

The horses had been fed with the last of the grain and the men ate salted deer meat off the spit. Richard Andersson was amazed at the freshness of the water in America and found that he needed much more to quench his thirst than he had in the past; he needed more food and rest for energy as well. His hair was lighter as he was clearly aging for the first time in hundreds of years. Jack could see it and Richard could feel it.

They had finished their food and now smoked quietly across the fire from one another in silence, when suddenly a wolf began to howl from a place up above and off in the distance.

"The wolves have found their way inside the canyon," Richard stated.

"I reckon they have found the crevasse," replied Jack, looking up in the direction from which the howling sounds emanated. "I do believe our tail is back, I just wish I knew their purpose in all of this."

"I have seen with my own sight that the wolves are not welcoming to the vampire," said Richard, "the enemy of thy enemy is not surely thy friend?"

"If you are sayin' the wolves can't be trusted, I see your meanin' from your strange talk, brother."

Jack and Richard both drifted off to sleep without setting one to guard over the other, for they had been on alert since they had left the Black Mesa Mountain, but for the first time in weeks they felt safe inside the walls of the canyon knowing the wolves were far off, allowing them to let their guard down briefly. Whether by luck or fate the old warriors managed the best sleep this night without incident.

Preacher Jack woke an hour before the sun to a pleasant surprise; sitting with his legs crossed at the fire was Chief White Owl, quietly smoking his long pipe. Jack sat up and crossed his legs in the Indian style with a grin on his face that had not showed itself for some time. Colonel Richard suddenly sat up and got to his feet putting his hand to the hilt of his sword and taking a step back in a prepared stance.

"At ease, soldier," said Jack, "this here is White Owl, Chief of the Navajo people; I would also call him teacher and my guardian angel in this war for the fate of the world."

Richard did not move and the Chief said nothing; he just stared into the fire while puffing on his pipe.

Jack could not help but laugh a little along with a smile as he said, "I see your skills of small talk have not changed any, there, Chief."

Jack brought his attention back to Richard, who still stood in his same position staring at the old Indian with a look of amazement.

"Richard, please sit," said the Preacher, "he is here for a reason that we will for sure find interestin'."

Richard relaxed a bit and sat down slowly, but did not take his eyes from the Indian—who looked magnificent with the large white headdress made of feathers he wore upon his head. He had seen this Indian from a distance once before, but up close the man was even more stunning. His perfectly tan skin and muscle tone was unreal for a man of his years. Richard could feel the power of his strength and the goodness radiating off of the old red skin.

"So, how the heck are yah, Chief?" said Jack, still grinning.

White Owl handed Jack the pipe while he said. "You have done well Preacher, but the fallen one has only just begun."

Jack grabbed the pipe; he took a few puffs and handed it back to White Owl. "Yeah, I kinda' figured that out, Chief, my dreams have told me just that. This here is Colonel Richard Andersson, somehow we are kinfolk."

The Chief looked at the Colonel for the first time. "I know who he is; there is still darkness in him, vampire blood runs in his veins and his heart struggles between good and evil."

Jack looked at the Colonel. Richard said nothing. Jack said in his brother's defense with honesty.

"Yeah, well, all of us struggle with that from time to time."

"He is here for a purpose that only the Holy Spirit knows," said the Chief, as he then handed the pipe to Richard; he accepted it and took several puffs and then handed it back to the chief with a nod of thanks. The tobacco was sweet yet slightly harsh, like a mixture of tea and pepper. Chief White Owl stood just as the sun was rising in the east.

"Come, we must reach the tombs before the sun sets this day."

"Before the sun sets?" asked Jack, as he and Richard stood and began to strike camp for the journey. "It's Andelko, isn't it, his head lives."

"The head has found a new body," replied the Chief as he mounted his horse. "He is forming an army as we speak."

With this said, Jack and Richard wasted no time preparing for the road. They set out with the old Indian chief who led the way toward the north as the sun marked the day.

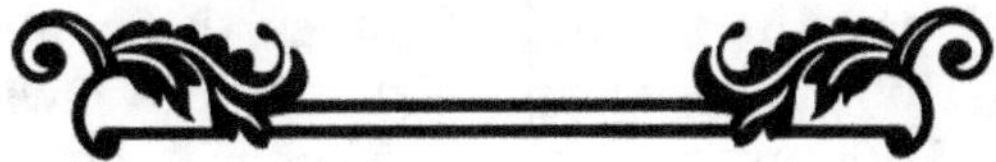

CHAPTER THREE

Revelation 6:8
*And I looked, and behold, a pale horse, and his name
that sat on him was death, and hell followed after
him, and power was given unto them over the
fourth part of the earth, to kill with sword, and with
hunger, and with death, and with beasts of the earth.*

Andelko Balas was now the Chief of a demon warrior
tribe that was one hundred strong. In life, the young
Apache Indians were some of the fiercest warriors ever
to walk the face of the earth; now, in death, they were
also completely evil as vampires of the undead and a
new coven.

The fallen one who was condemned to the bowels of
the earth refused to wait for the souls that awaited him
on the surface of the upper world. He was determined
to re-write the book of Revelation and rule before his
time. The spirit of the White Owl and Jack's renewed
faith had defeated Satan's vampire army on the top of
the Black Mesa Mountain; he had underestimated the
good soul of the Preacher. The Devil was responsible
for the death of Preacher Jack's wife and child in an
attempt to break his faith with God, but the Angel
Gabriel had sent his form, Chief White Owl, and
successfully rebuilt his faith that had turned to
victory.

Andelko Balas had recovered and reclaimed a new
life in a new body and an army with a new strategy

that could re-write the scriptures that would release the Devil upon the surface of the earth for a thousand years. At this moment only Chief White Owl, Colonel Richard Andersson and Preacher Jack Denton Anderson stood in the fallen-one's way.

The Apache vampire army was on the move, heading deep into the canyon. The first forty of Andelko's vampires were on horseback and the rest followed on foot. They were armed with tomahawks and fangs that killed with the strength of the un-dead; they also had other powers that had never been seen before. Chief Andelko, with his new Indian body, led his army of one hundred from the back of his horse through the paths and crevasses deep down inside the canyon of grand, searching for an artifact that was powerful and very, very, old.

It was late afternoon before any of the three men had said a single word. Chief White Owl came to a ledge at the end of the trail and came to a halt, allowing Jack and Richard to come alongside him. Jack looked around to see that the only passage way was to their right, between two narrow rock faces that led downward; he gave the old Indian more than enough time to speak, while he surveyed the bottom of the canyon that lay hundreds of feet down.

"What is it, Chief?" asked Jack "We been travelin' all day but this ain't the best spot for a campsite."

White Owl said nothing, he just continued staring down and into the gorge. Jack glanced at Richard, who also said nothing as he too was taking in the beauty of the landscape. *Great!* thought Jack, *I'm travelin' with a couple of deaf mutes, wonderful.*

"Are we at least close to these tombs, Chief? It will be dark soon."

"We are near," said the Chief. "Look there, Preacher, across to the other side." White Owl pointed down into the canyon. Jack's mouth dropped a little as he saw the line of horses appear into their sight. They were just specks at this distance, and traveling in the opposite direction, for which Jack was pleased because he could clearly sense the evil that was Andelko.

"My old Master Andelko Balas." said Richard aloud.

When Richard said this, Jack swore he saw the leader at the front of the traveling army turn his head and look up in their direction; this gave Jack a slight chill that ended in goose bumps.

"How many?" Jack said.

"The number is one hundred," replied the Chief.

"How in your God's name can we defeat that?" asked the Colonel.

"I have a better question," said Jack. "How are vampires travelin' during the day, can you answer me on that one, there, Chief?"

"Day-walkers," he said plainly.

"Day-walkers, what in the Hell is a day-walker?" The preacher received a look from White Owl that suggested that the word Hell was blasphemous but appropriate. "Meanin'?" Jack continued. "Vampires that can roam in the daylight, one hundred of um?"

"I have heard talk of these day-walkers back in the old country," said the Colonel, "it was said to be a myth, even among the undead."

"Well. brother, there's your myth right down there, God help us," Jack said as he made the sign of the cross on his chest. The wind suddenly picked up slightly.

"Come," said White Owl, "we must prepare."

The chief turned his horse and began the descent down into the crevasse. The Preacher and the Colonel followed.

The vampire army continued on in their search south for a holy treasure that had been hidden here for nearly two thousand years, since the Romans destroyed Jerusalem. Chief White Owl, Jack and Richard continued the short distance north to their destination.

The tombs were a cave system deep inside the inner cliffs that was once the home of ancient peoples. Ancient Hopi Indians were the most recent dwellers of the thousand caves that were formed throughout the Grand Canyon. In these current times only stone mummies dwelled here, carved out into the walls that reached heights of a hundred feet with Egyptian hieroglyphics imprinted into the rock. There were underground rivers and springs throughout the caves that were said to pass into the underworld and then connecting with the Nile in the land of Egypt. Here is where Chief White Owl, his twelve braves and the Navajo women were preparing for the second battle against the evil one, Andelko and his vampires.

Preacher Jack and Richard Andersson were clearly in awe as they entered the Tombs of the Ancients. This underground area was the largest of the caves. The men looked up inside the mountain walls; there were cut-outs in the embankments that slanted backward at an angle of about 35 degrees in two rows of three. Inside these were tiers of stone-faced knights with shield in hand; with the other hand they held a sword laid across their chest over a red cross, each one occupying a separate hewn shelf, six in all. They seemed to loom over a rock pedestal in the center of the floor of what appeared to have once been a coliseum.

"Who are they, Chief?" asked Jack.

"Ancient warriors from long ago," said White Owl. "They have been put to rest here in honor. They once were protectors and guardians."

Richard asked, "Protectors of what?"

"It is said they were raised to guard the priests and treasures from the Holy Land—so say the legends. There were once thousands of these knights in the Holy Land, these six were the last. "

"Well, it's a shame they are dead, for we could sure use more soldiers about now." Jack said.

"In my experience, Preacher," said the Colonel, "death is sometimes an illusion just waiting to rise again in another form."

"I git what you're sayin'," replied Jack, "this coming from a soldier hundreds of years old who might be my brother, who was once a vampire from across a great sea. Then you got the Chief here, who might be an angel or a ghost, I ain't sure which. The only thing I can be sure of, at this time in my life, is I should believe just about anythin'."

The Chief continued downward on the stone path until the ground leveled out directly below the crypts. They dismounted and observed the goings on. Twelve braves were hard at work carving arrows from straight wood, and several squaws were working around two camp fires, melting silver into bullets.

"These are the Indian warriors that followed my procession and then attacked my soldiers at the ravine in the desert." This was more of a statement than a question from the Colonel.

"I reckon that's right," said Jack, "like the Chief here, they are not much for conversation but they are good to have around when the fightin' begins." Jack looked toward his Romanian brother.

"I will be honored to fight by their side." Richard stated.

Jack acknowledged the Colonel with a nod and then walked over to one of the Indian women who sat with her legs crossed at the fire; she glanced up at him and he gave her a smile, for he recognized her from the last battle against the vampires. She was one of the squaws working in the hogans in the desert camp at the base of the Black Mesa Mountain. Jack picked up one of the silver .45 caliber bullets that were mixed in with .44's and rolled it between his thumb and forefinger; they all had a cross carved in their tips. He then spotted a wooden box full of ammo that rested behind her. With several strides Jack went to the box; he bent down and removed the largest bullet that he had ever seen. He then turned to the Chief and held the casing up high.

"Where is the gun that holds this shell, Chief?"

White Owl turned and looked in the direction of an Indian brave who stood to his right and twenty feet further back into the cave. Without any words exchanged the Indian removed a tarp that covered something set to the side among the shadows. Jack walked further back into the cave to get a better look.

"Holy mother of God," Jack said, "where in the world did you git these babies, Chief?"

"Like the silver sword you carry, the one that once protected the garden in Eden, the weapons appeared to me from the dust, a place I was drawn to deep into the desert."

Colonel Richard Andersson walked over to where Jack stood; the two Gatling guns' barrels shined in the flicker of the fire light. Richard had never seen such weapons, but with little observation one could see the destructive power that they held.

"I'm startin' to feel like we just might stand a good chance with this fire power," said Jack with some enthusiasm.

"Look here, Colonel, as fast as you can turn this crank right here," Jack grabbed the handle and began to turn it quickly, the clicks echoed off of the inner walls as the barrel turned; Jack had to raise his voice to be heard, "This model has six barrels—in the Civil War I seen the blue coats cut down my southern brethren like shootin' fish in a barrel, and with bullets made of silver with the crosses cut into the slugs, they will make good as vampire killers, day or night."

Jack stopped the turning of the guns handle that quieted the echoes that resonated off the walls of the huge rounded cave.

"I am impressed," said the Colonel, "you Westerners are quite efficient in the art of war."

"I hope you are right about that, Colonel, 'cause we are fightin' a different breed of vampire than before. We will not have time to rest under the sun. Day-walkers, shit!"

Jack looked over at White Owl—he stood tall, showing no emotion, as usual. The Chief was staring down at the rectangular stone mount at the center of the cavern. Jack could not help but notice that his headdress seemed to flow even though there was little or no wind inside the cave.

"Do you have anything to add to that, Chief?" Jack asked.

"The fallen-one is becoming desperate as winter approaches. His power slightly weakens with the cold."

"Then why not wait him out until the changing of the seasons, and then make our attack?" suggested the Colonel.

"The master vampire and his demons are in search of an ancient holy treasure, that if destroyed may change the fate of humanity."

"What is this treasure, Chief?" Jack asked, but before he could get an answer a ruckus could be heard near the entrance of the cave. Jack pulled his revolver and cocked the hammer with his thumb; he did this more with instinct than with thought. Jack had noticed that the colonel had pulled his pistol from his belt; Jack made a quick mental note that they must update Richards's outdated foreign weaponry to hold the bullets of silver.

Two of White Owl's Navajo braves came down the stone ramp with a prisoner. His hands were fastened with chains, and Jack noticed that the clasps around the wrists were forged of silver. The hissing sound the prisoner made sent chills up Jack's spine; he was getting very weary of this feeling he kept getting in his back. The Apache vampire was thrashing about with teeth bared and eyes that were black. Chief White Owl walked up to the day-walker and said to him in his Native American tongue. The vampire talked back with guttural growls in-between his words in a strange version of the Apache language.

"Preacher," White Owl called to Jack with a wave of his hand asking him to approach them, "he must speak the truth to the holder of the blue light."

Jack holstered his revolver and faced the Apache vampire, the sword on his back and the cross on his chest began to glow with the blue light. The Indian vampire tried to back away as he growled in the strange speech; Jack did not understand the outlandish language but he did understand the tone, it was a sound that was on the other side of righteousness. This creature reeked of evil; Jack fought hard to keep from losing his stomach. The possessed Apache suddenly became quiet and locked eyes with Jack and then he slowly said in English with the same low, guttural growl. "You will die, Preacher, and your soul will burn in the Hell fire."

Before Jack could answer the chief said.

"The sun, it sets."

How can he know this buried deep inside this cave? This thought ran through Jack's mind, but he knew better that to question the chief and after a second thought the timing seemed right for the ending of this day.

The Apache vampire changed quickly with the night fall into something that was not of the surface of the earth, but into an abomination from deep within. The odor of sulfur mixed with the smell of rotten flesh filled the area as wings made of grey skin broke through the back of the vampire. The chains that held the Apache dropped from his wrists as the body changed into a demon-like creature, its face contorted into something like a gargoyle with three inch fangs and claws like spikes. The demon growled as it took flight inside the cave; Jack pulled both revolvers and began to track the demon. Firing the silver bullets, he hit the target three or maybe four times out of the twelve shots as he spun and fired into the shadows. Jack holstered his empty pistols and pulled the sword of silver. The Navajo braves were firing arrows from their bows and hit the demon twice, bringing it down to the cave floor. Jack ran over to it as it flopped around and emitted a horrid scream; Preacher Jack put his boot on the neck of the devil's spawn and rested the tip of his sword on its chest where a heart should have been. The preacher said out with a booming voice, and his words echoed off the cavern walls.

"The wicked have drawn out the sword, and have bent their bow, to cast down the poor and needy, and to slay such as be of upright conversation. Their sword shall enter into their own heart, and their bow shall be broken."

The sword of silver flashed with the blue light as Preacher Jack thrust it into the demon's chest; the demon quickly turned from gargoyle, back to vampire, and then into the Apache for which he was born before turning to dust from which he had come. As the light diminished, one Navajo brave walked over to the pile of ashes and retrieved Jack's silver slugs and the two arrows. Jack sheathed the sword that hung from his back.

"You reckon' I could take a look at that?" asked Jack, while reaching out for one of the feathered arrows. The brave handed it to him and watched as Jack inspected the tip. It was made of silver and had crosses engraved on both sides. Jack handed it back with a nod of approval and turned to White Owl; the chief had not made a move since the vampire had changed into a flying demon and attacked them.

"One down and ninety- nine to go. I take it they all change at night?" asked Jack with tired concern.

"Vampires that walk by the day and demons that fly by the night," the Chief replied.

"That's great," said Jack, "day-walkers and flying demons, suddenly the Gatling guns have lost some of their edge."

Richard walked over, with his sword in one hand and his cap-and-ball pistol in the other. He spoke as he joined the two men.

"We will need an abundance of the silver ammunition for the big guns, as the flying demons' flight speed is great and erratic."

"In the bowels of the cave," said the Chief, "is a vein of silver. My braves will work day and night mining and making more bullets of silver for two days and then we must move on, no later than two days."

"Why two days, Chief, what's the hurry? Where is Andelko goin' and what is he up to?" Jack said. "Help me out here Chief, 'cause this guessin' shit is wearin' me out."

"The master vampire is searching," White Owl said.

"Searchin' for what?" Jack asked.

"He searches for a holy treasure, a powerful treasure that was meant to save but only cursed."

"Cursed who, Chief, us or them?"

White Owl shrugged his shoulders. "All of humanity, Preacher, only time will tell you these things."

"Wonderful, two days then," said Jack, as he then turned to Richard. "The first point of business for you, Colonel, is we have to find you a new sidearm that shoots the silver .44 or .45, what you got there ain't gonna cut it in this war."

"I had a set of the western guns once," said Richard, "but they seem to have been lost, where I do not know."

Jack dug through the supplies at the back of the cave and found Richard a set of forty-five Colt revolvers and a yellow boy Winchester rifle acquired by the Navajo braves, along with as many silver bullets as he could carry. The colonel politely requested a large amount of silver to be melted in a trough that he chipped with a mason's skill out of a ledge of a rock formation. A fire was built underneath the thinned out rock to melt the metal, into which he then dipped his bronze sword. He then leaned his shield against the stone trough and, with the cast iron pot, he dipped out and then poured the remaining liquid silver onto the outer side of his shield, coating it with the vampire deterrent. In the process of his forge work, Richard had carelessly splashed a small amount of the liquid silver on his forearm; it naturally burned but quickly cooled into hard little droplets. Jack was there with him, and their eyes met as Richard peeled the dry metal from his skin.

"Well, brother," said the Colonel, "the skin burns as it should, but not long ago this metal would still be eating away deep into my flesh."

Jack reached up and placed his hand on the shoulder of his long-lost kin that he now called brother.

"Restorin' your humanity was the easy part, my brother, makin' a believer outta of yah may take some more time."

They were twelve Navajo warriors and their Chief, a preacher cowboy and an ancient soldier; they were preparing to take on a more powerful evil than they had defeated at the Black Mesa Mountain, a wickedness not seen since the days of Sodom and Gomorrah.

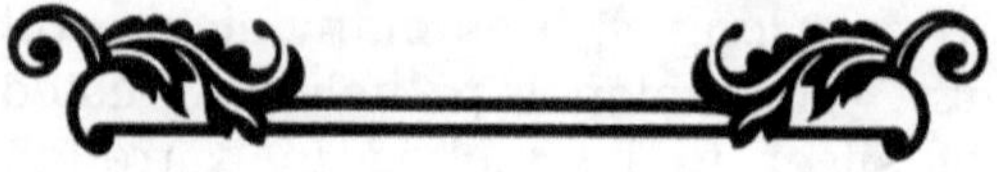

Chapter Four

Genesis 4:14, 15
*So the Lord said unto the serpent. "Because you have
done this, "Cursed are you above all the livestock
and all the wild animals! You will crawl on your
belly and you will eat dust all the days of your life.
And I will put enmity between you and the woman,
and between your offspring and hers; he will crush
your head, and you will strike his heel.*

The master vampire Andelko Balas, who was now occupying the body of the Apache Chief, led his army of day-walkers through the massive canyon of grand in the search of God's law. Chief Andelko had been summoned by his master, who was known by many names: Satan, Lucifer, Devil, Beelzebub, and the fallen angel who resides deep within the bowels of the earth. It was here that Andelko was then given his orders, as he had traveled in a perpetual free fall for what seemed like days to face his master. Andelko Balas was the Devil's serpent; like the snake which deceived in the Garden of Eden.

Satan preyed on the un-believers, on the weak and the insane, to do his dirty works on the earth until the time when he could live on the surface and reign as king of the sinners of the human race; Satan was once an angel under God, until the Lord asked him to bow down unto Adam; the angel's pride would not allow it, so for his defiance God sent him downward to rule the fires of Hell until the written time of Revelation would come to pass. The fallen angel had grown impatient over the thousands of years while he was locked away as a prisoner in the Hell fire; he was desperate and would once again try to rewrite the history of man.

Andelko had new life and a new body which allowed him to walk among the living in the daylight as a vampire, and the ability to change into a winged creature in the night. The army of Apache warriors was under his total control; their dead black hearts were easy to rule, as their souls had been captured by the fallen-one. Andelko was given the freedom of spirit to do Satan's bidding and he did so willingly, for his lust for power infested his soul.

Andelko and the demon army were in search of signs of an ancient guard; the guards that Andelko sought where much older than he, they were men of ancient times around the year of 1100 A.D. The Knights Templar guarded treasures and knowledge and protected Christians throughout Europe until they were disbanded by France in 1312 and were unjustly charged with heresy and accused of homosexual acts. Thousands of these Knights were rounded up and stripped of their White robes marked by the Red Cross; they were tortured into confession and then burned to death at the stake. The ones that escaped did so with God's treasures and scattered to lands all around the world, including lands as far away as North America.

Andelko Balass was searching for the caves of the Knights Templar where a great power had been hidden, a divine power brought over on ships from the Holy Land. Destroying the laws of man could change the history of man, by then changing man's fate. Andelko's orders were clear and he would carry them out at all costs.

Chief Balas stopped his horse and slid from his mount with grace, floating down to the rocky ground of the canyon floor. The Apache day-walkers obediently came to a halt and formed a defensive posture around their master as he studied some ancient carvings on a rock face that he was drawn to. Andelko's new Indian body was different than the one from his turning, but it was coming into its own. He recognized his bony fingers as he brushed sand from the grooves of the writings; he found he had the ability to change his appearance at will. The ancient writings were written in code. Andelko could not interpret what they said, but the symbol he sought told him it was of the Knights Templar. The hooked X was used throughout the script. The top part of the X was said to symbolize the womb in its upward v shape, the bottom of the X symbolized the penis pointing upward like an upside down v and a hook at the top of the x symbolized the child. Andelko did not know if Jesus had spawned a child and he did not care of the son of God's possible blood line, what he cared about was carrying out the fallen-one's orders; and those orders were to find one certain powerful treasure that the Knights had sailed to America to hide.

All the hooked X's among the writing suddenly glowed with the blue light that forced Andelko to throw his hand up and cover his eyes in a defensive posture; he took a step back and slowly removed his hand from in front of his face to see that the writing on the rock had returned to normal. Andelko stepped away from the rock with an evil grin and said with conviction,

"Your powers are weak here, Jesus of Nazareth, for this is not the majestic Temple of Jerusalem or the Mount of Olives, this ground is not holy, this is the desert of the west where men have forgotten of your promise to return."

Andelko and his army moved further south, looking for more signs of the hidden treasure of old. Andelko was guided by visions when he concentrated on the object that held the tablets. There were forces of good surrounding the artifact which held a white light that blocked its whereabouts, but at times his master's evil would break through and send Andelko on the right path. The vampire Chief mounted his horse, preparing to continue on following the river that flowed at the bottom of the canyon, when he suddenly felt a presence that he had not felt in some time; it was his childhood friend and the Colonel of his past army. His name was Richard Andersson. Andelko could see through the Colonel's eyes—there was a blurred figure of a man that cleared for a moment. The word "Preacher" escaped Andelko's thin grey lips as he recognized the man.

From across the desert, at that very same instant, the Navajo chief called White Owl stepped between Jack and Richard and into Andelko's view as if to protect the preacher; the chief's eyes shined blue and disrupted Andelko's spying vision.

"*So,*" thought Andelko at that same moment, back to the south, "*I still hold some power over my Richard and he is not mindful of this. The one called White Owl is from the heavens and he is aware, I will have to choose my prying time wisely.*"

Andelko's thoughts were powerful and he looked to his turn-lings closest to him in search for a telepathic response; there was none. Andelko suddenly realized he was alone in this war, for the Apache demons were powerful soldiers but they had lost their souls. When a man is turned from human to vampire his soul is not lost but only changed, but when men are turned to demons they must lose their selves completely; Andelko regretfully missed his old coven and the days when he ruled Drazan Castle in the country of his birth. He especially missed his old friend Colonel Richard Andersson; at the very least, he yearned for his conversation. Andelko was searching for the Ark of the Covenant that held the tablets of God's law and was once carried by Moses. Andelko realized for the first time that he would have to do go it alone, for there would be no one by his side to share his soon to-be-victory.

Meanwhile, across the desert in the Tombs of the Ancients, the army of good discussed a new discovery.

"What is it?" the Colonel asked White Owl, who had quickly stepped between him and Jack and was looking at Richard strangely.

"Your eyes for a moment were not your own," replied the chief.

"What are you sayin', there, Chief," Jack asked, interrupting the conversation and walking around to White Owl's side to face Richard.

"Your Colonel's eyes glowed red and he did not know. Andelko looked upon you, preacher, through your brother' we must be aware of this."

"I lost some time," said Richard. "I sensed a loss of control of my actions when he looked through me. I will work on resisting him, but we have been connected for so long I do not know if I will be successful."

"You need to find a way to turn the sight within, like a two way mirror of glass, and see what he sees," Chief White Owl explained.

"Turn the tables on um," said Jack, "reverse the sight on him and see what he sees, can you do this, Richard?"

"You ask much," he replied, "but I shall try."

"Chief, I know you like to keep me guessin', but I'm askin' you straight, what is Andelko searchin' for?"

White Owl looked directly at Jack and said, "The Tablets of Moses."

Jack mouthed what the chief said without sound, his brow looking confused; *The Tablets of Moses.* "The Ten Commandments?" said Jack aloud. "The Ark of the Covenant?

The Chief said nothing, he just looked at Jack with his emotionless stare. Jack suddenly realized that the old Indian always looked very clean and without sweat; his feathered head dress seemed like it had just been crafted.

"What in the... Heck... is a four thousand year old script from the Holy Land doin' in the Americas? No, scratch that. What is God's word doin' here at the bottom of the Grand Canyon in the Arizona desert, for Christ's sake." Jack was beginning to pace back and forth now as he said.

"Who are we to question God?" said White Owl.

"I'm not questionin' God, I'm askin' you, Chief," said Jack with his hands held up in the air with frustration. The Chief answered with the most words at one time that Jack had ever heard him speak.

"A long time ago in the land across the sea the Knights with the Red Cross worn on their clothed chest were formed to protect the church and its treasures. They were great warriors of God until the new king of France was influenced by the evil-one and the king rounded up the knights with his army and tortured confessions from them, confessions of heresy and homosexuality. The Knights were then burned at the stake to their death. Some of the Knights Templar got away with the sacred treasures of the church, but they were forced to leave their homeland and head out to sea searching for a land known only by the Vikings."

"When I was a boy I heard stories of the Knights Templar," said Richard. "They were brutally disbanded by King Phillip the fourth of France. There were rumors that some escaped to Scotland, but I never heard that they sailed as far as the Vikings, it was taught that Columbus discovered America many years later."

"Well, thanks for the history lesson, gentlemen," said Jack, "but I'm afraid two days won't do, this changes everything—we must leave at first light. Andelko's got a head start on us, that's ok by me, for

I'd rather sneak-up on um from behind anyhow. Your braves, are they ready, Chief?" Jack asked.

The Chief nodded ever so slightly in a downward direction indicating that the answer was yes. "The braves will work through the night making silver bullets for the big guns."

"It will have to be enough. What about you, Richard, are you ready to ride into the lion's den?"

"Prepared and as keen as I could ever be, Preacher, if good and evil are not prepared to fight their own battles than I presume we will have to do it for them." The colonel said this with vigor.

Without another word said, Preacher Jack then went off by himself and found a place to bed down against a rock wall deeper inside the cave. He was completely exhausted. If the demons came tonight they would win this war, for Jack did not have the energy to fight back nor did he care. He lay down and placed his Stetson over his face purely out of habit, for there were no stars or moonlight shining inside the mountain cave to conceal. He then set the sword of silver on top of his chest; he closed his eyes and began to pray until he fell into a deep sleep.

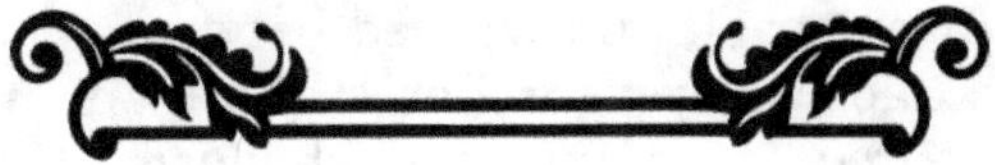

CHAPTER FIVE

Psalm 46:4, 5
There is a river whose streams make glad the city
of God, the holy place where the most high dwells.
God is within her, she will not fall; God will
help her at break of day.

The morning sun shone bright into the canyon over its giant walls from the east, bringing on the day and lighting the way for the army of good. Chief White Owl was on point; the Colonel was riding behind him and third in the line rode the Preacher. The twelve Navajo braves followed behind them single file with their weapons of silver and the horses pulled the two wheeled Gatling guns by their hitches.

The terrain at first was difficult to maneuver when leaving the entrance of the caves, especially for the gun's wagon wheels, but as they descended to the bottom of the canyon the ground leveled out and widened for easier travel south. They had traveled deliberately and without conversation for many hours when, just past noon, Jack spotted something to his right and across the river bobbing between some rocks in the shallows. Without a word Jack left his rank in line and guided his horse into the stream for the other side. The depth of the water came to Jack's knees and near the shoulders of his stallion; the current was swift but manageable for the animal and they reached the other side fairly quickly. As Jack got closer he could see that there was a body of an Indian woman floating on her back and wedged between two rocks at the bank. Jack shored his horse and dismounted and took the three steps into the shallows. He put his fingers to her throat, searching for a pulse; he found one, but it was very faint. Richard and his Clydesdale had followed Jack across the river and now came alongside him.

"Is she alive?" he asked from atop his great horse.

"Hardly."

"Do we have time for compassion, Preacher?"

Jack looked up at the Colonel and said nothing, but his gaze said much.

Jack noticed this squaw was a mixed blood, maybe twenty years old and extremely beautiful. He reached his arms underneath her body and picked her up; he carried her up the bank to a grassy dry area and laid her down softly. Richard tossed him a rolled-up blanket from the back of his horse; Jack placed it under her head. She began to stir with a moan and then slowly opened her eyes; they were a lovely green color that seemed brilliant, set off by her copper-colored skin and her long jet black hair.

"Who are you?" she asked.

"You speak English, that's good; this will make things much easier. Are you hurt?" Jack asked.

She began to try and sit up; Jack helped her slowly to her feet. She was wearing a short brown suede skirt that was one piece that strapped over her shoulders. It was soaking wet and water dripped from the rawhide fringe. Jack looked her over and found some blood at the back of her head were there was a small cut on a pretty good size knot.

"What's your name, ma'am?" Jack asked.

"You say it first," she answered.

"Sorry ma'am, my manners have been lost out here in the wilderness for some time, the name's Jack Denton Anderson."

"Preacher Jack Denton Anderson?" she asked.

Jack had forgotten the cloth he wore around his neck for a moment as he greeted her stare with a smile.

"I am called Lina," she told him with a smile of her own.

"I do not mean to intrude," said the Colonel, "but we do have a schedule to keep that is of the upmost importance."

The mixed blood woman looked up at Richard on his great horse, noticing him for the first time, and then she looked back at Jack with an expression of confusion.

"Believe it or not, that there is my brother Richard," said Jack. "I know he talks funny, but you'll git use to it. He is right, though, we must git movin'. You can ride with me and we will hear your story when we set up camp in the evenin'. "

Richard Andersson had already maneuvered his Clydesdale easily through the river and was waiting for Jack to bring his new passenger across, doubled up on his stallion. Richard was alongside Chief White Owl as they both watched Jack's slower progress.

"Do you know of this woman, Chief?" asked the Colonel.

"She is a Navajo half-blood, braves take white woman in raids and battle and make them part of the tribe, giving birth to half children."

"I wonder," said Richard "is she a friend, a foe or just happenstance?"

The Chief looked at the Colonel with question, "I do not know this word."

"Happenstance, it means by chance," Richard explained.

"She is not chance, there is no chance in these times, and everything has meaning." said the Chief, "only time will tell what her purpose will be, for good or for evil."

"It has been my experience that women seem to walk that fine line between good or bad and bound from side to side to appease their own benefit."

"Yes," agreed the Chief, "they are one of God's most wondrous and sought-out creations."

White Owl's definition of a woman made Richard Andersson smile with a slight chuckle, which was a rarity.

"Are we smiling, Colonel?" questioned Jack with irritation as he moved the stallion in his place in line. "It is not often that talk with the Chief here brings humor, anythin' I should know about?"

"Not at all, Preacher," said Richard, "we were discussing wondrous creations. That is all."

"Well, if you boys are done, we need to move out," Jack commanded.

With a nod of agreement from Richard, Jack slipped in behind White Owl, who had already begun to move on, creating a space. The half-blood squaw gave Richard a look as they passed by him; for an instant she thought she saw the Colonels eye's change color.

The Army that held the power of the blue light moved at a steady pace following the river back to the south in the same direction as Andelko and his day-walkers. The canyon of grand seemed to widen as they traveled; the sun was non- existent as the low moving purple and black clouds now covered the sky like a low ceiling. Lina twice turned her head to look into the eyes of the foreign Colonel from the back of Jack's horse. Richard peered back without expression, like two lovers might do to hide a secret. No one said for hours until Chief White Owl put up his fist with his arm bent to signal a stop.

"What is it, Chief?" Jack asked as he pulled back the reins on the stallion.

"The night approaches, there is a large cavern up ahead in the rock where we will camp."

"It's not that I don't believe yah, Chief, but how do you know that?"

"You have to be an Indian to know these things," said the Chief. To Jack he sounded a little boastful.

"Yeah," said Jack with a roll to his eyes, "but you're right, we don't want to git caught out here in the open at night if we can help it, lead the way Chief."

White Owl led them away from the river about a mile to a cliff face that had a deep overhang that funneled into a cave protecting them from three sides and from above. The braves set up most of the camp talking only to White Owl and only talking very briefly. They were wonderful soldiers, they never complained about their duties nor did they need much to accomplish them; they were some of the fiercest masters in the art of war that Jack had ever seen.

Richard, White Owl, Jack and Lina sat and ate potted meat in silence over a small fire while the braves were on the watch and in their defensive positions in case of an attack on the camp. Jack was the first to finish his meal, for he was anxious to ask questions of Lina. He pulled the last of his rolled cigarillos and lit one with a burning stick from the fire. Jack breathed in deeply and then exhaled as he looked to the half -Indian woman who sat with her legs crossed, staring into her now empty bowl. She glanced up at Jack, feeling his gaze upon her; she looked away bashfully and then set her bowl down. When she did not speak, Jack decided he would have to initiate the conversation.

"Lina, can you recall how you ended up where you did on the side of the river?"

"Yes I...I ran." She paused as if trying to collect herself. "I awoke early in the morning with my little sister; her name is Aiyanna, *was* her name. It was still dark and we wanted to surprise mother with some fish, so I went up river and Aiyanna went down river. I had to travel far to a pool that was a known fishing hole, I was surprised to see it was empty. When I was returning there came many screams from my village so I ran toward it and I saw—" Lina stopped and covered her face with the palms of her hands as if to block the image from her mind. After a moment she continued, with anguish building in her voice. "The men of my village were eating the women and children and I saw my father just standing in the middle of it all but his face had changed, no that is wrong, not his face but his entire head was not his."

Lina talked as if she clearly did not understand what had happened to her people, but White Owl, Jack and Richard understood completely and if this woman lived long enough, eventually she would too.

"Then what did you do, Lina?" Jack asked with care.

"I turned and ran the way I came, and I kept on running, and then I fell and I must have hit my head, and then you found me."

She was clearly shaken; Jack handed her his smoke, which she took and puffed several times. She then reached out to hand it back to him, but Jack raised his palm in a gesture for her to keep it.

"You are of mixed blood." This was a statement and not a question from Richard. "How did you come to live with the Navajo?"

"My white mother was taken on a raid and made a slave in the beginning; one day Chief Hoskininni took a likin' to she and they were joined. It was my father's body I saw in the camp, but his head was not his own."

Lina dropped the cigar and covered her face with the palms of her hands once again but said no more.

After a long silence Chief White Owl said.

"Chief Hoskininni was a great warrior; he would not surrender to the blue coats during the relocation. Hoskininni means angry one. The Navajo tribes were forced hundreds of miles from their land in what is known as the Long Walk, the Apache refused and took their people and set out for new lands. It seems they settled here in the canyon of grand."

Jack stood and removed his hat; looking like a man of faith, he placed his hand over Lina's head and bowed his own.

"He sent from above, he to me, he drew me out of many waters.

He delivered me from my strong enemy, and from them which hated me; for they were too strong for me.

They prevented me in the day of my calamity, but the Lord was my stay.

He brought me forth also into a large place; he delivered me, because he delighted in me."

Lina looked up to Jack, "Thank you preacher."

Jack made eye contact with her and smiled. He placed his hat upon his head and walked away from the fire, his back fading into the shadows as he went deeper into the dark cavern where he planned to slumber through the night.

They would all sleep or rest in different degrees according to their respective needs. Jack would crash, as he was exhausted; he figured Lina would sleep, for he assumed and hoped she was human like he was. His brother Richard still had vampire blood within him and was a soldier hundreds of years old and he would rest in his own way. The Chief and his braves, as best Jack could tell, were angels or ghosts; they seemed to replenish themselves very little. Jack hoped this night would be a peaceful one for they would all need their rest moving forward.

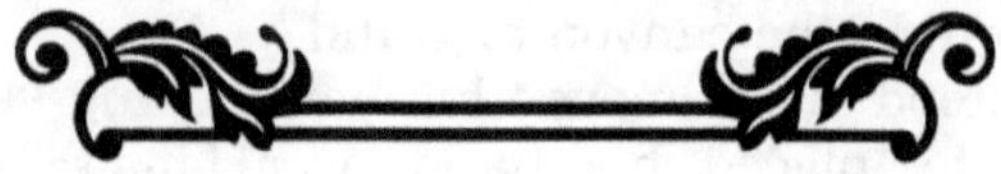

CHAPTER SIX

Luke 10:3
Go! I am sending you out like lambs among wolves.

She came to him in the early morning darkness at the back of the cave and woke him with a kiss. Jack wrapped his arms around her and pulled her on top of him; they were very close and then he rolled Lina over onto her back. The kiss was passionate and extremely deep. Jack pulled back and their eyes met for a short moment; she smiled at him with love in her eyes and then in a split second the eyes turned red and her face changed, her smile was filled with jagged teeth and yellow fangs as she lunged into his neck...that's when Jack awoke, sitting up quickly as a bead of sweat rolled down his cheek. He was breathing hard and waiting for his eyes to adjust to the dark cave, he made the sign of the cross on his chest with his right hand which immediately stabled his nerves. Jack looked down and to his right to see Lina asleep three feet from where he lay; her features were amazingly beautiful even in the dim light. Her eyes opened and Jack was relieved to see that they were colored green and not glowing in the demon red.

"Is it time to travel?" she asked.

"Time means nothin' here in the dark. But my inner clock tells me the sun is not yet up—but yes, soon."

Jack got to his feet and, with his fingers, he combed his brownish hair back from his face which had grown long and was seemingly out of control. He placed his hat upon his head and rubbed his face stubble which made a sandpaper sound. Lina had rolled over on her side and appeared to drift back into sleep. Jack had slept fully armed and he now adjusted the weapons to their rightful place. He then walked away from her toward the diminished fire to see Richard stretched out with his eyes closed. Jack turned and took two steps, making his way to the entrance of the cave when Colonel Richard's voice stopped him in his tracks.

"Our food supplies are low; we must hunt, if we become pinned down in a battle for a considerable amount of time what we have for nourishment will be depleted quickly."

"I agree, Colonel, we got a few hours before the sun, let me talk at the chief and then we'll go see what we can shake outta the brush."

Jack found White Owl standing in the moonlight just outside the cave entrance where the rock over-hang began to open wide; he looked like a statue staring straight ahead. Jack wondered how long he could stand there completely still.

"Mornin', Chief, I don't know about you and your braves but us mere humans need to stock some meat before we move on."

"What man needs the White Spirit will provide," the Chief replied without turning his head or changing his stance.

"Yep, I git that," Jack said, "but the Lord only helps those who helps themselves; and us mere men gotta eat."

"When you return from the hunt we will head to the south on the heels of the enemy." White Owl said this as Richard Andersson stepped out from behind them and into the open; he was fully dressed and armed with his sword and his holstered revolver hung from his hip. "I am ready, preacher, shall we depart?" he said as he walked on toward where the horses were corralled.

"Let's git to it, the moonlights a-wastin'," said Jack as he followed the Colonel and left the Chief to continue with his statue routine.

The two men were on a hunt like brothers might do on a normal day in a different time and a different place, which made Jack feel ordinary for a moment, locking all thoughts of their mission now to the south deep in the back of his mind. Richard was all business, but he did feel a bond growing inside him for this man called Preacher Jack.

They did not have to travel far to find an oasis of forest down in a ravine near one of the many creeks that broke off from the main river. Jack quickly found fresh mule deer tracks that stopped at the water's edge and then returned after a drink and then backtracked into the woodlands. Jack and Richard dismounted. Being as quiet as possible, and tied off the horses to the branches of a giant cottonwood. Jack pulled the Winchester from the saddle's scabbard and unloaded the silver bullets and replaced them with standard lead ammo. The lead was more accurate than the silver, and the silver would be wasted on a hunt for anything other than vampires.

"We should have brought along one of the Chief's braves, their bows are much quieter than this yellow boy rifle," Jack whispered as they followed the prints deeper into the thicket along a small path. It was an hour before sun-up, but the sky was now cloudless and the stars and moon were shining bright, giving off ample light. A twig snapped up ahead and to their right, bringing the two men to a halt; Jack slowly moved some tree branches aside with the barrel of his rifle, revealing a large clearing were a spotted doe was chewing new grass covered with early morning dew. Jack cocked the lever action as slow and as quietly as possible and then aimed the rifle's sights high on the neck of the female deer and squeezed the trigger The cracking sound of the Winchester echoed loudly through the woods. The mule deer jumped to the side and took off at a run, attempting an escape; the doe made it to the middle of the clearing before hitting the ground, dead and silent.

"Got um," said Jack excitedly as he left the tree line toward the kill. Richard began to follow and then stopped in his tracks. He looked around, sensing something lurking in the crisp, clear air.

Jack reached the downed animal; he went to his knees, laying his rifle on the ground, and pulled his knife from the sheath.

"She's a good size for a doe, brother, and will go a long way."

Jack said this thinking Richard was right behind him, so when he heard rustling at his back he thought nothing of it at first. Something in his mind alerted him when more sounds of moving brush seemed to surround him, from his front and from his back and moving to his sides. The clearing that Jack was settled in was the size of a half-acre and was well lit with moonlight, but the thick foliage growing in-between larger trees that encircled the clearing held darkness. Clouds seemed to come out of nowhere suddenly and blanketed the sky. Jack froze as he saw red eyes appear directly in front of him just inside the tree line—moving his head slowly he glanced to his left, where he spotted another set of eyes and then quickly to his right. Two more red eyes appeared.

"Richard?"

"I'm here at your back, Preacher." The Colonel said as he slowly unsheathed his sword; it made a sliding metallic sound, alerting Jack. The sword of silver was slung over the preacher's back, and he did not want to make such a broad move for removing it from its sheath. The eyes that were directly in front of him began to move forward and toward him. Jack's hand slowly went to the butt of his revolver.

"I'm gonna' stand now," whispered Jack, "how many?"

"I have two directly at our rear; you have the one up front, there are two more at our flanks, one left and one right. That would be five," replied Richard with some surprise to his voice, *Five? It cannot be*, he thought.

The wolf pack had the two men surrounded as they deliberately left the thicket and moved slowly toward them and into the clearing. They were in the stalking position, teeth bared and head held low; all at once they began to growl from deep within their bellies as the hairs on the back of their necks stood firmly straight up.

The preacher and the colonel were both standing back to back now. Richard had his sword pointing forward and his other hand had slowly drawn his revolver and he now pulled the hammer back with his thumb. Jack had sheathed his knife and now had both his pistols pulled; the clicking sounds that the hammers made as he drew them back stopped the forward progress of the wolves.

"The white is the leader," Richard said. He knew this even though he had not turned to look. "He is the key, and the others will not make a move without orders from their commander."

Jack could feel the cross that hung around his neck begin to warm with the blue light. He slowly slid his revolvers back into their holsters, leaving them cocked, and then pulled the glowing cross out from under his buttoned shirt. The white wolf immediately went to the sitting position; the other wolves followed. Their growls quieted and their teeth vanished behind their closed snouts.

Jack slowly pulled his sword from the sheath that rested on his back; it shined blue, but the glow was dim as if it was only warning and not showing its full power. Jack said directly to the white wolf as he stuck the sword into the ground between the lead wolf and the deer that lay still at his feet.

"I feel your hunger, great one; I am the Preacher and if you will let me carve this animal we may share this meat in a cease-fire."

There was a short pause that seemed much longer than it really was, when Richard said over Jack's shoulder.

"What did he say?"

Jack turned his head to answer in surprise with his brow furrowed and his mouth slightly agape, as the colonel appeared to be making a rare joke.

"Really, now you find a sense of humor? I'm gonna bet since this animal has not attacked me yet it means we understand each other."

Jack realized he should not have taken his eyes off the white wolf, and thanked God he was not at this very moment being eaten alive. With the sword of silver glowing blue between him and the white wolf, Jack pulled his twelve-inch Sheffield from his belt and kneeled to begin the letting of the deer's belly. He kept one eye on the leader of the pack as Richard stood protecting Jack's back. The carving of the deer may have been some of Jack's best work; it was definitely his fastest labor. As long as the dim blue light radiated from the sword all was quiet, allowing Jack to do his butchering. He wrapped the meat that he would keep into a blanket for the carry back to camp; normally he would salt the meat directly, but under the circumstances that must wait. He left the front legs and the back legs along with the carcass to the carnivores that patiently waited; the only movement from the wolves was the panting of their tongues. Jack grabbed the hilt of his sword and used it as a crutch to pull himself up to his feet. When he stood the blue light ceased; the black wolves began to growl and bare their teeth once again in unison.

"I purpose it is our time to depart, Preacher." Said the Colonel with urgency; this was the first time he had said a word since he had said in jest.

"If you mean git the heck outta here, I would agree," Jack replied as they moved slowly through the gap between two of the black wolves at their back. Jack kept his attention on the white wolf who sat there calmly staring directly into Jack's eyes. As he and Richard departed, they held their swords out in front of them in a defensive position. The black wolves circled around and met at the center of the clearing and began to feed on the carcass of the mule deer, allowing the two men to escape back to the trail inside the brush. Jack and Richard quickly mounted their steeds; the howl of the white wolf could be heard throughout the canyon, spooking the horses, but they were able to control the mounts and flee back the way they had come as the sun threatened to rise in the east and begin a new day.

CHAPTER SEVEN

Ezekiel 22:27
*Her officials within her are like wolves tearing their
prey; they shed blood and kill people
to make unjust gain.*

Jack and the Colonel had wasted little time getting back to where White Owl and his braves were waiting patiently on their mounts packed and ready to move out. Lina was now sitting upon a white colored foal of her own as one of the braves rode a new wild, apparently just captured. Jack was especially happy to see Lina, who seemed more familiar somehow, even more beautiful than the last time he had seen her just a short time ago. White Owl and Richard both noticed how the Preacher shined when he saw her, which concerned them slightly. After a moment, Richard noticed something different about her; Lina seemed to be more stunning than before, like she had captured youth somehow. The Colonel made a mental note to keep a closer eye on her as he was not very trusting.

Jack quickly salted and stored the meat from the mule deer into several saddle bags. They would not have time to eat, for the army must move on; the last of their jerky would have to do and be consumed from the back of a moving horse.

The trail widened out an hour down the road, allowing Jack to ride up alongside the Chief who was leading their way. Richard followed and rode up beside

Jack to be part of their conversation; Lina stayed back, but was in ear shot and the Colonel noticed that she was listening and at the same time pretending not to do so.

"Chief, me and the Colonel here ran across a pack of wolves on our hunt this mornin' and they have been tailin' us for some time." Jack waited for White Owl to reply. As usual he did not, so Jack continued. "The pack is led by a larger white male and when I looked into his eyes there were smarts there that I have never seen in an animal before."

White Owl moved forward silently, as if Jack had said nothing. Irritation was building up in Jack. He was not in the mood to play these games so early in the day, as he was about to snap. Richard said up and cut him off.

"Chief White Owl, these wolves are somehow from my homeland for I once witnessed them battling with some of Andelko's coven, by some means they crossed the ocean and followed me here to America, this I cannot explain."

"I know of the white wolf, he is of middle world," said the Chief, "he does not fight for the good or the evil but only for himself. If help or hurt comes from him and his pack it will be for his wants, not ours."

"How did this creature come to be?" asked Richard.

"The white wolf was once an angel of God, as were his pack, who had fallen out of favor, they were after a time also rejected by the evil-one, they were turned into wolves and condemned to roam the earth in solitude."

"Does this white wolf have a name, Chief?" Jack asked.

"His angelical name was Dantanian, which means he who appears as a man with many faces. As a fallen angel he was called Marchocias and he once commanded thirty legions of demons, until the prince of darkness condemned him and the others to animal form. Marchocias hoped after hundreds of years to return to heaven with the angels and become Dantanian once again, but he may be deceived in that hope. It is said that under request the white wolf changes shape into a man."

"This is good to know," said the Colonel, "when we cross paths again I will make the request."

"No,' said the chief, "only the Preacher can ask of this."

"Great!" said Jack. "More of that chosen-one crap. You know I got a half a mind to just to ride on outta here and just keep on goin' and leave you angels and demons to figure all this out on your own. You know, life was a hell-of-a-lot easier when I just wanted to soak at the bottom of a whiskey bottle."

As soon as Jack said this he regretted it; he glanced back at Lina, knowing she had heard their conversation.

"Never mind me, let's just git on with it."

Jack said this as he steered his horse to the lead, not waiting for the others. They followed without a word spoken for some time as the sun rose straight up, marking high noon. Jack needed a drink more than ever, and as he would soon find out, the Lord did work in mysterious ways.

The braves followed their leaders quietly, hauling the two Gatling guns. All were armed with the bullets and the arrow heads that had been forged in silver. The tomahawks they carried were also dipped with the shiny powerful metal. Colonel Richard Andersson's blade and shield were dipped in silver and Preacher Jack's sword was of the ancient silver that once guarded the entrance to the Garden of Eden. The Sword had the power of God in the blue light along with the cross that Jack wore around his neck, laid over the collar of the Preacher. The collar protected his neck and the cross shielded his heart. The only true protection that sheltered Preacher Jack Anderson's spirit and soul was the strength of his faith, which at times wavered.

The road they traveled led them some distance away from the river. The rushing waters could still be heard but only when all were stopped and quiet. After a time White Owl had taken back the lead point from the preacher; the chief looked up to see buzzards circling in the sky and off to their right. He gracefully steered his horse off the path back towards the river. Richard and Jack followed; Lina did not, as Jack motioned that they would be right back. She and the braves stayed behind in wait. Jack noticed once again that the braves seemed to know what to do without being told.

They came around the corner of a rock formation where it opened up at the river bank to reveal what was left of a camp. There was a wagon with two mutilated horse carcasses still connected to the yokes and spread out along the ground. As they dismounted and walked around to the other side of the wagon they spotted what was left of two men in the shallows. Their bodies were torn apart and decapitated, and the river was red with blood. They had dismounted and walked to the shallow part of the creek on foot.

"Well, it appears we are traveling the correct route," said Richard as he knelt down by one of the dead bodies with his sword drawn. He used the tip of the blade to move around the clothing and revealed bite marks covering the dead man's flesh. Richard then walked four feet away from the body to poke at the head; he rolled it over to see the last expression that the frontiersman would ever have, one of sheer terror.

"There are many bite marks, too many to count and the head is severed, ripped off, the neck is completely gone," Richard yelled.

Jack was at the other body down river from the first. "Same here," Jack yelled back, "but this man's head is missin'. I suppose it could have washed down river?"

Jack and Richard left the bodies and met up with White Owl at the wagon where he stood with his back to them. They came around each side of the Chief to see what he was staring at; on the bench seat of the wagon was the missing head sitting upright on its chin, for it was cut high on the neck. The mouth was stuck open in a soundless scream and upon the head set a worn Stetson. The chief reached out and removed the hat to reveal a message scratched in the forehead; blood red letters simply spelled: 'PREACHER'.

"Like I said, we seem to be traveling on the correct route," the Colonel said with little emotion.

"Andelko," said Jack, "he left this here for me. Well, that answers a question, he knows we are followin' him."

White Owl said, "It is written: for he cannot destroy God's law on his own, only a priest can survive in its presence, or in this case a Preacher."

Jack's rage built up suddenly and he back handed the head, sending it off its perch and into the river. "If he thinks I will help him destroy mankind he's in for one big ass revelation 'cause this time I'm gonna kill that son-of-the-devil once and for all."

Richard placed his hand on Jacks shoulder, "And I will be right there by your side to assist you, brother."

Jack walked around to the back of the wagon and began going through the small stack of supplies. There was some coffee and sugar stashed under a few blankets, and behind that was an open wooden box. "Jackpot!" he said as he pulled from it several bottles of whiskey and a pouch of tobacco.

"Jackpot? And your name would be Jack," said Richard. They both looked at one another and Jack managed a smile. The newly found brothers looked over at the Chief. He stood looking back with that same emotionless expression, which made the two men laugh. Jack pulled the cork and took a swig with half of it running down his chin; he handed it to

Richard who took a long draw before handing it back. Jack paused for a moment and then handed it toward the Chief, who did not take it, he just turned and walked to his horse and mounted.

"Well, Richard, I don't think dad approves," Jack said, trying to hold back a chuckle.

With a smile from Richard, "We best go, brother, evil awaits."

The two men grabbed up the supplies, mounted their horses and met up with White Owl and the rest where they waited on the path. Jack looked up at Richard sitting upon his Clydesdale. "Damn that's a big horse," Jack said, just before taking a long draw from his bottle. Jack was joyful for the first time in a while, but that soon went away as he glanced in the direction of the river and up at the circling buzzards.

"Hold up Chief." White Owl turned his attention toward the preacher as Jack spoke to him.

"These men need a proper burial."

"It is being taken care of as we speak, Preacher," replied the Chief.

Jack looked over his shoulder to see that two of the Navajo braves were gone.

At that very moment two braves had dismounted at the river's edge and began collecting what was left of the mutilated bodies and placing them in the wagon.

Jack took one more swig of whiskey and then corked it. He kissed the outside of the bottle and then stashed it with the others in his saddle bag. They began to ride out. Jack looked back to see a cloud of smoke billow up into the sky; it was not a burial but a cremation, which was acceptable. Jack was glad they were up wind and away from the smell of the burning flesh.

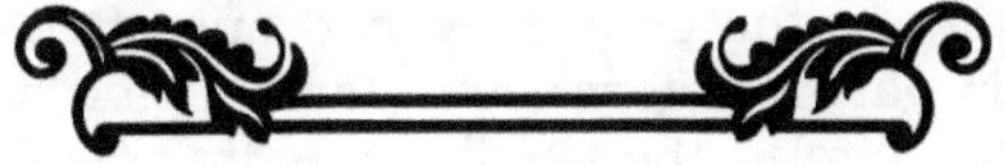

CHAPTER EIGHT

Revelation 13:11
*Then I saw another beast, coming out of the earth. He
had two horns like a lamb, but he spoke like a dragon.*

The sun had set in the west and the darkness took
over the canyon. Andelko stood above his army of day-
walkers, controlling them with his power and not
allowing them to turn into the flying demons that the
night brings. It took much effort for Andelko to do this,
for it was the demon's nature to change with the
coming of the night; their purpose was to feed and
become an army of destruction and horror. Andelko
was being called from deep within the earth by his
master and he knew he would lose control of the
Apache vampires as he descended deeper into the
passage way to meet with the fallen-one. Every
creature with a heartbeat and pumping life-blood
would be devoured by the gargoyles within an unknown radius until the chief vampire returned to take
back control of their feeble minds.

The heat and smell of rotting flesh laced with sulfur
grew as Andelko reached the passage way to Hell deep
inside the mountain; he still had control of his army
throughout the cave, but as he looked down he saw
the bottomless pit and he knew he would have to
release them. Andelko closed his eyes and jumped into
the dark pit; he descended feet first with great speed
straight down. After several minutes in free fall

Andelko could hold them no longer and the army of day-walkers in the canyon turned one after the other into their gargoyle form and took flight looking for blood. They circled the sky like the dragons of the east and then dove down and devoured their own horses that were scattering at full speed erratically in a panic. It was a despicable massacre on one of God's most wondrous creatures, but as the horses perished one by one, their spirits could be seen running in bliss up into the heavens, they were covered in the soothing blue and white light that released them from their evil capture once and for all.

Andelko was unaware of what was taking place on the surface as he was still in free fall into the depths of the earth. The bottom of the dark hole was now lit with the color of fire as he was getting closer to where his master resided. Andelko's descent took thirteen minutes by the clock; when he hit bottom his left leg bent, landing on its knee, and the other leg landed on the moccasin covered foot, where his elbow rested. Andelko's head was down in a submissive bow as the hot dust shot up from his landing and swirled around in its own wind. When the dry, sulfur dust cleared, Andelko opened his eyes, but he did not raise his head for he would wait for his master to speak and release him from his yield; the evil-one would do this when he pleased and not a minute before.

Andelko Balas was many hundreds of years old and in that time he had rained down terror on human kind ever since his turning. This was only the third time in his long life that he had felt fear, and he did not like it. The first time was when he was attacked and turned into a vampire, the here and now in the presence of the fallen-one was the third. The second was the first time he had met with the beast in the cave at the Black Mesa. Andelko had not had contact with his master since he had lost the battle for the earth at the Black Mesa Mountain where the Preacher had cut off his head with God's flaming sword. He had failed, and now he would either get a second chance or his dark father would surely send him down further into the hell fire to be tortured for eternity?

Speaking in an ancient tongue made up of Aramaic and Hebrew, the evil one's voice was booming but also low and guttural; the speech echoed off the rock walls.

"You continue to disappoint me, Andelko. I made you and gave you great power from the black seed of my loins and I allowed you to sit as a king. When it was time I returned to you and set you upon new lands, I set you upon the path of evil perpetuity upon this earth."

"Yes, Master," replied Andelko—the sound of defeat could be heard in his voice.

"Lift your head and look into my eyes," demanded the Evil One; as he spoke a swirl of fire grew behind the rock throne that he sat upon. Andelko raised his head and looked upon his master; the horns that protruded from each side of his head were tipped black with blood and his long fangs dripped the nasty liquid constantly. Andelko beheld Satan's glowing red eyes that were hollow and bottomless; he was pulled deep inside them where he could see the souls of the damned being tortured forever and a day. Andelko could hear himself screaming in the distance, and then he was suddenly released and back in the underground mountain with his maker, a split second before he would have gone completely mad.

He was the Fallen-one that had turned into a serpent and counseled Eve in the Garden of Eden; he had turned Cain against his brother Abel and tempted Jesus in the desert. He now used some of that same manner of persuasion with his turn-ling.

"Now that you have seen what will become of you if you fail me once again, perhaps you will succeed, for I have given you a new body and a more powerful army of demons at your command."

"Tell me what to do, my father and master of the underworld, and it will be done," Andelko replied, still on one knee. His foreign but familiar head looked forward, but never ever again would he look into the eyes of the father of evil.

"Find the Ark of the Covenant that contains the ten laws," growled Satan, "the ones in which the creator wrote—you must destroy them, but you cannot touch or look upon the tablets or you will surely be destroyed."

"Forgive my ignorance, Master, but how can I destroy something I cannot touch?"

"Only the Preacher can touch or look upon Gods laws, not even the White Owl can do this."

"Why will the Preacher, this chosen- one, why will he help us take over the souls of humanity?" Andelko asked reluctantly.

The fire in the room flared up, making it unbearably hot but ice cold at the same time as the devil with many names shot fire and smoke from his nostrils in a fit of rage; a black and green blood-like substance leaked from his serpent looking eyes as he growled, "Must I recognize everything? Can you not find some answers on your own with the powers I have bestowed upon you? This will be your last chance, Andelko Balas, if you fail me you will burn in my Hell for eternity!"

"Yes, Master, consider it done."

"Now depart from me, and I will not set my eyes upon you again until we are both on the surface and standing in victory," the Devil said, calming somewhat.

Andelko did not hesitate in the slightest; he backed his way to the opening that led to the surface above and began to climb the rock walls very quickly, like a bug or gecko might, with ease. As he got closer to the surface and farther away from the enemy that was his maker, his fear subsided and Andelko was again his ruthless self. As his powers began to grow and the dark sky became visible, Andelko took flight and soared to the surface. He landed feet first on the rocky ground; the chief vampire looked down at his boots to see horse carcass surrounding his ankles. He surveyed the area, seeing the winged demons feeding on what was left of the horses' flesh.

"Mindless minions of dis, heretics and pagans they are, I am left upon this cursed earth to deal with such incompetents." Andelko growled this with disgust.

The White God had freed his hoofed creatures of the earth from their enslavement, not allowing their souls to be consumed by the beast. Andleko could not fathom how a God so powerful felt the need to show compassion for a dumb animal like the horse. He smiled with confidence, for this was the White God's weakness: the love for his children, man and animal. His love for his creations would be his undoing. So believed Andleko as he regained control of his demon army with a simple thought; they flew down and some walked awkwardly from where they were feeding and lined up as best they could in their current form. The Gargoyles snapped at one another as their wings opened and closed, each irritating the one next in line, they were like evil unruly children; with a command from Andelko the winged creatures changed into their Indian vampire form for the march. If only Andelko knew their destination they would then fly there quickly, but he needed to travel by ground and search for the signs left by the Knights Templar.

The Lord and Master of the Devil's army would not be reduced to marching on foot, but the vampire gargoyles had devoured his horse, so Andelko dropped to one knee and prayed to his creator Satan, known as the deceiver that leads humanity astray; the ground shook and split apart as a black horse rose through the rock. The beast wore a saddle made of human skin with spikes made of bone that draped down his four muscular legs. The stallion was the size of the Clydesdale and he breathed fire from his nostrils like a dragon. Like the angel changeling that was the giant white owl on the side of good that once flew with Andelko's head in its talons, the black demon horse was just the opposite, a fallen angel changeling on the side of evil.

Andelko mounted the dragon-like horse and began his march in search of the Ark of the Covenant that contains God's ten laws of commandment. Somewhere hidden in the vast canyon was the gold-laden box with the Cherubs upon it; Andelko would have to find a way to trick the Preacher into destroying the tablets. If he did not find a way to win this war he would surely suffer an existence that even a master vampire could not endure.

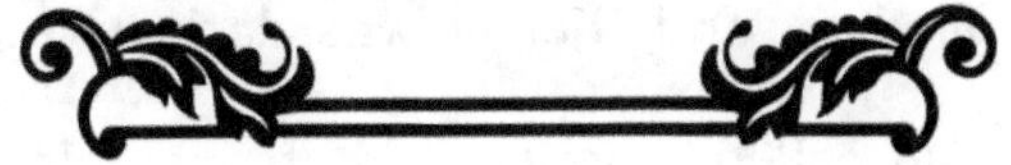

CHAPTER NINE

Job 39:19
*Hast thou given the horse strength? Hast
Thou clothed his neck with thunder?*

Jack did not sleep well this night. The thoughts of the severed head robbed him of much needed rest, not to mention the cries of terror that he now heard off in the distance. Lina and Richard had awakened when the sounds of a slaughter echoed across the canyon valley. Jack was already standing and facing the direction of the commotion, and the silver cross he wore around his neck was clutched firmly between his thumb and forefinger.

"Are those the screams of animals?" Lina asked as she walked up beside him.

"Horses, I think?" said the Colonel as he walked up on the other side of the preacher. Lina gave Richard a look that said she did not appreciate the interruption, Richard gave her a look back that made her turn away.

"Well, it sounds like death," she said, "I should have been killed with my people. Preacher, tell me, why was I spared?"

"That is a question for the Chief," answered Jack, "he seems to always know more than he's talkin', maybe you should have a pow- wow with him."

The cries suddenly stopped and the quiet that followed was deafening for some time. Then black clouds quickly formed in the distance and blue lightning lit up the sky. The canyon reflected blue and white in a series of flashes, and then it was dark as night once again.

"This land called America is a strange place," Richard commented.

Jack turned to look at Richard, taking his eyes off of the sky to the south for the first time since he had stepped onto the ledge.

"You're comparin' the strangeness of this land with yours—where you come from you were once a half-vampire soldier, hundreds of years old and living in a castle, you protected a coven of blood suckers in the daylight hours, and you call this place strange? I'd say you fit right in around here, my brother."

"I see your point, preacher, my whole existence has been extraordinary and even more so as the years pass by, and I do believe all lands are strange in this day and age." Richard said this with some awe in his voice.

Chief White Owl was suddenly standing there just behind the three of them and looking to the south, slightly startling everyone.

"Chief, I wish you would quit sneakin' up on me like that, at least give a warnin'." Jack complained, sounding more like a cowboy than a preacher.

"The spirit horse has been released into the heavens, only the flesh left behind to be devoured by evil. The army of the underworld travels on foot for a time," said White Owl, ignoring the preacher's complaint.

Jack quoted John 10:10 in his preacher voice. "The thief cometh not, but for to steal, and to kill, and to destroy; I am come that they might have life, and that they might have it more abundantly."

The Colonel spoke directly to White Owl, ignoring Jack's sermon and moving on to the business at hand.

"They do not need horses to travel, for in the darkness the vampires turn and take flight like the bats of the night."

"Your former master does not move in haste for he does not know where to find the gold box that is God's word. He seeks signs left by the Knights Templar to guide him and waits for us to overcome him."

"Overcome? You mean to catch up with him?" the Preacher asked.

The Chief nodded, his feathered headdress blowing in the breeze.

"Well," said Jack, "we will oblige him. I say while we're up we might as well git an early start."

They all agreed without a word and walked from the ridge to strike the camp. An hour had passed and the sun was yet an hour from rising by the time they mounted and moved out. The lightning storms had calmed for the time being, and it looked to be the start of a clear day, which pleased Jack. Though the new breeds of vampires were day-walkers it still felt as if the sun could give them an advantage.

It was high noon when the following army of good came across the rock with the hooked X. The tracks they followed told them that someone had dismounted here and inspected the writing on the wall. Jack knew it was Andelko that had been standing here; the preacher's boots were in the vampire's tracks and he could sense the evil that had tainted the sand. Richard had dismounted and was by Jack's side; he could feel Andelko's presence as well. It was stronger here than he had felt in sometime.

"I recognize this text," Richard explained, "mostly this." He placed his finger under the hooked X pointing it out in several places. "I have seen it on carvings in my home land, it is very old."

"The language is ancient," said Jack with some confusion. "It's difficult to believe this is here in America, in this canyon, it's downright impossible if you ask me. These Knights sure did git around."

"Is that so, you use the word impossible," Richard replied with surprise.

Jack made eye contact with Richard, who was giving him a look of dismay.

"Yeah, I reckon not impossible," said Jack, "at this point I should believe anythin', but my teachin's left out some hefty figures. I would have liked to have met these Knights Templar, for I have many questions."

"Careful what you request, Preacher, for you might just receive such bidding."

"If you mean careful what you wish for 'cause you just might git it? Well, I git that," Jack replied with a small grin.

They kept riding, leaving the rock to weather in the elements for another thousand years. Jack was eager to catch Andelko and his army, but at the same time his good sense told him to turn and run the other way. He took a long draw from the whiskey bottle, immediately triggering a need for a smoke. The preacher drank and smoked as his mind wandered, for something told him that in the end he would have to finish this on his own. His thoughts were interrupted by a slow rumble of thunder that could be heard across the sky. Jack looked to the heavens and spoke from memory, the Book of Psalms 20:6.

"Now know I that the Lord saveth his anointed; he will hear him from his holy heaven with the saving strength of his right hand.

Some trust in chariots, and some in horses; but we will remember the name of the Lord our God.

They are brought down and fallen; but we are raised, and stand upright.

Save, lord; let the king hear us when we call."

Peals of thunder rumbled louder at the finish of the scripture spoken by the preacher. Colonel Richard had a sudden feeling in his heart that he had never felt before. It only lasted a second, but it seemed to open his mind to this God that he had never known.

Richard looked to Lina; she seemed totally unaware of any goings on; this bothered Richard. *So God does not speak to this woman,* he thought to himself with suspicion.

They had traveled all day and the night was sneaking up on them quickly as the bottom of the sun could be seen threatening to collide with the horizon. The Chief spotted the wolves off in the distance. The line of horses came to a halt; as they did, so did the line of wolves in the light of the setting sun. They were a mile away and very small, but you could see the larger white wolf leading the black ones. The wolves turned toward the army of good with the sun at their backs and their hind legs bent as they took to a sitting position three feet apart and lined up in a row. Even at this distance the horses seemed to sense danger as they, too, were turned and facing the pack.

"What are they doin' Chief?" Jack asked.

"They wait for the setting of the sun and the rising of the moon," he replied.

They all watched the wolves as the setting sun disappeared behind the rock wall of the canyon in the west and then was replaced in the east by the rising of the moon. The eyes of the wolves could be seen in the new coming darkness. Suddenly the glowing eyes disappeared as their heads went back and the howls of the wolves began, echoing throughout the canyon of grand. The horses spooked; as Jack fought to keep his stallion under control the clouds cleared and the light of the full moon came shining through. The howling stopped and the wolves were gone.

"Like I had mentioned," said Richard, "this is a strange land."

"These are strange times," said White Owl, "the un-written times, the Fallen-one wishes to write his own book to replace Revelation, and this must not come to pass."

"Don't you worry, there, Chief, for I'm the chosen one, remember." A hint of sarcasm could be heard in Jack's voice. "We best set up camp for the night and git some shut eye, 'cause late tomorrow we should catch up with Andelko and his demon army."

"Yes," White Owl replied, "I feel this will be so, many will die by this time tomorrow."

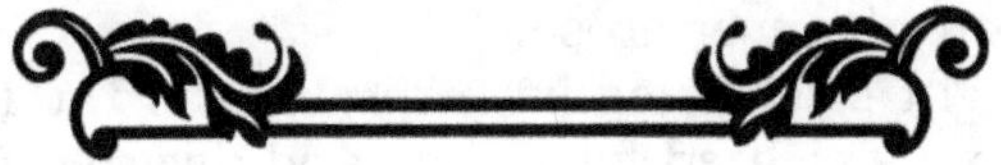

Chapter Ten

Exodus 31:18
When the Lord finished speaking to Moses on Mount Sinai, he gave him the two tablets of the testimony, the tablets of stone inscribed by the finger of God.

Andelko Balas and his army had been traveling day and night looking for the signs of the Knights Templar. The Ark of the Covenant would most likely be hidden deep in a rock tomb among the thousands of caves and crevasses throughout the canyon. Only the clues carved among the rock would lead them to its whereabouts, for not even the power of the fallen-one could pinpoint the location of the Ark. A shield of great power surrounded the gold-laden box and the legend told that only a chosen few could touch the ark and live.

There had not been any new symbols found since the last, but everyone in this action knew that heading south was the right direction. As soon as the sun went down, Andelko's extraordinary hearing picked up the howl of the white wolf far off in the distance. He pulled back on the reins of his dragon-horse and cursed the sky. Andelko knew of the spirit wolves that held alliance to no one but themselves, they were caught up in the middle between good and evil and Andelko was suspicious on what side of the conflict they would fall. He would not take the chance that they would ally with the Preacher, so Andelko made a decision at that moment that he would destroy the Angelical canines if the opportunity ever arose.

The night brightened with the light of the full moon as the clouds cleared for a time and diverted Andelko's attention to the terrain around him. He concluded that this would be a good place for an ambush of Chief White Owl's army of braves. Not one demon Apache would confront the Preacher as ordered by Andelko, but they would attack and mutilate all the others in the white chief's army as is their nature. This act would send the Navajo spirits back to where they belonged back to their resting place before they had meddled in his earthly affairs, so swore Andelko.

It was late afternoon the next day when Chief White Owl came to a halt at the top of a ravine that cut through the canyon rock. The terrain ramped down with cliff walls one hundred feet high on both sides about a half mile long and one hundred feet wide. Jack, Richard and Lina brought their horses to a stop alongside the Chief.

"You got to be kiddin' me?" pronounced Jack in disbelief. "You reap what you sow, look familiar to you, brother?"

Richard was quiet at first and stared down into the pass. "Very familiar, Preacher, the last time not long ago I passed through a gorge nearly identical to this one, and my army of Romanian soldiers did not fare too well, I alone survived."

"So we go around this valley of death?" Jack suggested.

"No," said White Owl, "this is the path south we must take, for time is short."

Jack ignored the chief. "Two days maybe three to go around. Shit! It's suicide to be caught down there, this gorge is a perfect site for an ambush. Hell, maybe Andelko moved on? What do you say, Richard?"

Richard's eyes had changed to a blood red color as he stared trance like into the canyon below; it took a moment for him to shake the infestation of evil. His eyes changed back. "I have done as you asked, Chief White Owl and turned the sight on Andelko, I saw through his eyes and he is here." The Colonel grabbed his forehead with some pain.

"I lost it, but I did see us standing here and now, the ambush is real."

The men were not paying attention to Lina, whose eyes had also turned red as soon as Richard's changed back to his own. She looked around suddenly, as she had lost time and seemed not to know what was going on; as she grabbed her forehead to soothe the pain, Richard saw her reaction and made a mental note. He now knew she was under Andelko's power at times, as was he.

"There will be no going around, for this will be the first battle of our journey," The Chief said without emotion.

"Ok Chief, but this won't be our last, if we are goin' in there we're gonna do it smart. Richard, you're the leader of armies here, what do you think? The braves go in first?"

Richard pointed. "We set up the big guns on each side of the ridge from the high point, with two braves pushin' us forward, and I will be firing a gun on one side and yourself firing one on the other."

"That is a good strategy, Colonel," the preacher agreed, reinforcing this with the up and down movement of his head even before the Colonel had finished.

"Chief, I ain't sure what to do with you, any ideas?"

"My destiny has already been written, Preacher."

"Yeah, right, you do whatever you do," said Jack with the bad habit of his eye roll, "let's do this before I change my mind. Lina." She was staring into the ravine. "Are you with us, Lina?"

"Yes, Preacher," she finally answered.

"You stick with me, I want you by my side at all times."

"No," said Chief White Owl, "she will stay with me."

"Ok, Chief," agreed Jack. He pulled an extra revolver loaded with silver from his saddle pack. "Can you shoot?"

"Yes," answered Lina, "my...father taught me long ago."

Jack handed her the weapon and then, with Richard in tow, they fell back to prepare the army. At first Jack was surprised when without a word from him the four braves were already moving the big guns to the flat ridge, one on one side and one on the other just as they had planned, two braves per gun as the rest began moving single file down into the ravine with bow and arrows drawn for battle. Jack had left Richard for the other side of the gorge.

It took twenty minutes for the men to reach their positions. Richard dismounted his horse and stepped on the metal platform attached to the back of the rotating guns as the Indians pushed him into position. Jack was on his platform observing the eight braves marching single file below, and he wondered if the Navajo warriors entering down in the ravine knew they were being sent into a meat grinder to flush out the vampires.

The sun was setting in the west, being replaced by the moon in the east; this night the moon had changed color to a blood red and was hanging low in the sky. The night would change the vampires into their demon form and they would attack from the air.

"Richard!" yelled Jack from across the gorge. "Aim for their bodies at center mast and then sweep the barrels upward toward the head."

Richard raised his hand acknowledging that he understood. At the top of the ridge, Jack mouthed a prayer aloud from Psalms. They waited for the demon army to attack.

"Lord, how are they increased that trouble me? Many are they that rise up against me.

Many there be which say of my soul, there is no help for him in God, Selah.

But thou, O Lord, art a shield for me; my glory, and the lifter up of mine head.

I cried unto the Lord with my voice, and he heard me out of his holy hill. Selah.

I laid me down and slept; I awakened; for the Lord sustained me.

I will not be afraid of ten thousands of people; they have set themselves against me round about.

Arise, O Lord; save me, O my God; for thou has smitten all mine enemies upon the cheek bone; thou has broken the teeth of the ungodly.

Salvation belongeth unto the Lord; thy blessing is upon thy people. Selah."

As soon as the preacher had finished the verse the sun completely disappeared behind the ridge forcing his eyes to adjust to the new light of the moon. The screeches that sounded like that of tormented animals could be suddenly heard over the flapping sounds of wings in motion, not feathered wings but wings made of skin. The first wave of demon vampires appeared from the outside of the ridge, flying up and diving into the gorge upon the Navajo braves who were now caught in the middle with nowhere to retreat. Jack began turning the Gatling guns and cranking the handle as fast as he could, aiming at the fast and erratic flying gargoyles. Richard was firing his big gun on the other side of the bank as the two braves in charge of his repeating weapon slammed the clips for the reload and wheeled the Gatling gun forward slowly. The second wave of flying demons rained down on the braves in the gorge. The Navajo warriors shot their arrows upward—they were surprisingly accurate, and fearless with their aim, but there were so many flying demons that some got through the defenses, decapitating some of the Indians or first taking limbs with claws that cut through bone like heated lard.

The first wave of attack caught Jack and Richard off their guard, but the second wave of demons could not escape the rapid fire of the big guns. The two soldiers of good were now comfortable with their weapons and to Jack's delight the large silver calibers were ripping the demons apart with flashes of the blue light. It was an amazing light show of power whenever a bullet came in contact with the flying devils. Jack was suddenly feeling cocky and made the mistake of allowing a thought to creep into his mind, *this is gonna be easier than I thought;* at that moment a third wave of demons changed direction and began to descend on Jack. He had to abandon the big gun and pull his sword; the blue light glowed bright as he cut through the bodies of two with one hard swing. The braves that pushed him along had to abandon their posts and were in battles of their own, shooting arrows in the air with great speed. Three more demons flew down on Jack, one after the other, but they were not coming in head-first for the kill but feet-first like a bird of prey. Jack realized they were trying to carry him off alive for capture; with four or maybe five swings of his sword the three demons exploded in a flash of blue light. Jack sheathed his blade and breathed heavily. He looked across the gorge to see Richard battling for his life; there were dead cold-ones piling up around him, and the braves by his side were taking others out in hand to hand combat with tomahawks dipped in silver. Jack yelled out to his braves by his side as he turned the barrels of the gun toward his left across the gorge toward Richard. "Keep them devil sons-a-bitches off me!" He began firing in a sweep above Richard's head, hitting his marks and splattering a shower of guts and body parts. Jack could sense claws grabbing at his shoulders, but he ignored this, having to put his faith in the fighting braves around him. Suddenly his ears were ringing as the guns' ammo ran out and there was nothing but a dry clicking sound. Up to this point the

Indians had been taking care of his reload but they were currently busy keeping the demons from carrying him off, so he scrambled to reload his own clip when there came a sound across the valley; it was a hissing shriek that Jack knew well. It came from the bellows of Andelko Balas, apparently calling to the gargoyles in an instant retreat as they began to flee.

There were piles of dead demon Apaches lying along the ridge around Richard and around himself as the live ones flew back from where they had come, from the outside of the canyon walls. Jack looked down in the ravine to see many dead demons along with the bodies of the slain braves; very few of the Navajo warriors below had survived the ambush.

A woman's scream came from behind Jack at the entrance to the gorge; *Lina?* Chief White Owl was finishing up with one last demon from the top of his horse; his tomahawk took the gargoyles head in a flash of white light. A demon had plucked Lina from her horse and was flying away with her shoulders locked in its talons; Jack yelled at the chief, who had already pulled back on his bow and was aiming the silver tipped arrow at the flying enemy.

"Shoot, dammit, shoot!" yelled Jack from his post. The demon went straight up and out over the outside canyon wall and went straight down, disappearing over the rock cliff. Lina's screams faded to silence. The Chief did not release his arrow.

Jack was not able to contain his anger, for he had let down too many people in the past, particularly the women and children close to him. He had mounted his stallion and at a very fast pace headed straight toward the chief who had disarmed himself and sat upon his horse in wait.

Huffing and puffing, Jack did not yell but talked through clenched teeth as he swung down from his mount. "Why the hell did you not shoot, Chief, you don't miss; you could have saved her!"

"I did save her," said the Chief in his practical, monotone voice, "she would have fallen to her death had I fired."

Jack suddenly knew the Chief was right, but that just infuriated him even more. The stare-down he was now having with the old Indian was one he knew he could not win.

"Son-of-a-..." exclaimed Jack as he pulled one pistol and slid to the ground from his mount. He made his way swiftly to the edge of the cliff; he looked down into the outside canyon for any sign of Lina. There was nothing but red colored darkness.

Richard came alongside the Preacher and followed his stare downward; unlike Jack, Richard could see through the red moonlight.

"Can you see any signs of her?" Jack asked.

"Sorry, Preacher, I fear not, but she still lives."

"How can you know that?" the preacher asked, needing to hear some words of hope.

"If they wanted her dead she would be torn apart and lying in a heap of flesh on this ridge, the fact that they seized her states they want her alive to use her against you."

"Yeah, that makes sense," Jack replied. He had not once taken his eyes from the bottom of the darkness since their conversation began.

"We need your attention at its fullest, Preacher."

Jack turned his head and made eye contact with Richard, putting on his best poker face. "Do we have a body count?"

The Colonel tilted his head toward were the Chief awaited on top of his horse and walked away. Jack followed.

"What's the damage, Chief?" asked Jack as he approached White Owl.

"In the forties the Anasazi demons have fallen."

"You call them Anasazi? Explain," the Preacher asked.

"In Navajo it means Ancient ones or Ancient enemies."

"How many braves did we lose, Chief?" Jack continued while Richard quietly listened.

"Six braves have moved on into the spirit world, leaving half of the twelve from the battle at the Black Mesa."

"Sorry about your loss, Chief." Jack was no longer upset with the old Indian and said this sincerely. "I will remember these courageous men in my prayers."

"They were resurrected to serve their purpose as was written, tears had been shed for them long ago."

Jack had a look upon his face that said *I give up.* Richard quickly spoke.

"I do not intend to grieve lightly, but we must bury the dead and move on."

Richard and Jack fetched their horses and met up with White Owl, who had moved to the edge of the ravine where they surveyed the bottom of the gorge. The Navajo bodies had vanished, leaving the Anasazi demons' remains scattered about the canyon floor, along with a dozen more or so at the top of both sides of the ridge around where the Gatling guns remained.

"A portion of our job has been completed," said Richard. "I feel no comfort in leaving the demon carcasses to be fed upon by the animals of this land."

"I reckon I agree with yah, brother, evil might still live in those remains. Got any plans, there, Chief?"

"It matters not, Preacher, what plans we shadow, God's plan has been in motion since the beginning of time. Witness, the light cometh."

Chief White Owl was directing his arm straight out with his open hand to the east as the first rays of the sun broke over the horizon with blinding waves of yellow. The demon bodies at the top of the ridge that White Owl referred to as the Anasazi instantly combusted as the beams of the morning reached them with the speed of light. The Anasazi carcasses at the bottom of the ravine began to smoke, slowly at first, and then more rapidly as the rays of light found them at the bottom of the ravine.

"Strange that the light comes early," said Jack, "by my clock the sun should not rise for another ten hours."

"The canyon of grand now runs on its own time, different from the rest of the earth." White Owl stated.

"Good to know," said the Colonel, "that the demons burn in the sun light."

"Flying demons yes, day-walkers no," said the chief, changing the direction of his arm to the south-east toward the next ridge some two miles off. There stood Andelko in the middle of a line of Apache vampires. The army of good had killed forty-odd of the one hundred Apache demon vampires. The surviving ones could be seen stretched out across the horizon. Jack scanned his enemies from left to right and then he set his sights on Andelko, who was glaring back at him, his red eyes visible even from this distance.

"Andelko Balas." The name escaped Jack's lips softly.

"Preacher," Andelko said simultaneously through clenched teeth, from the ledge miles away.

After a moment the once Apache Chief who now wore the head of an ancient vampire pulled Lina from behind his back and held her out by the nape of her neck with an extended arm. The vampire braves hissed in unison, creating an echo over the canyon. Jack's anger grew as he quoted scripture

"The Lord is my light and my salvation," said the preacher.

"Whom shall I fear?

The Lord is the stronghold of my life, of whom shall I be afraid?"

But Jack was afraid, he was afraid for Lina and angry at the same time. Somehow he suddenly realized that he had a connection with her, somehow his dead wife's soul dwelt in the half Apache squaw. His past was coming to light within him.

Andelko and his day-walkers, around sixty in all, stepped back and vanished over the ridge.

"We need to git movin'," said Jack, "daylight's a-wastin' and the days and nights are gittin' shorter, it seems."

Richard spoke sternly, stopping Jack in his tracks, "You must come to the realization, brother, that Andelko is using this woman to gain a strategic edge over this battle situation. I need to hear that you understand."

"Oh, I git it, all right," replied Jack. "I know now that long ago in New Mexico my wife and children and my whole congregation was wiped out by a disease brought on by the Devil, the same Devil that runs Andelko. Someone's gonna pay as long as I'm still breathin'."

Chief White Owl spoke with conviction. "If it is the redemption you seek, Preacher, it will only be achieved by your faith."

"Yup, I reckon, Chief, but right now I don't feel too faithful. Mow let's git goin' before I change my mind, 'cause Hell is where we're goin', there, Chief, and I'm gonna end this once and for all."

Jack guided his horse toward the entrance of the gorge, and Richard followed. After little conversation they decided to leave the Gatling guns behind, for there was not one horse left to pull them. Jack, White Owl and Richard sitting upon their mounts and the braves following on foot, they continued south as the sun was now being covered by a smoky mist; a storm was coming, and with it a bloody rain.

CHAPTER ELEVEN

Job 29:23
And they waited for me, as for the rain, and
They opened their mouth as for the latter rain.

Andelko Balas rode his Dragon horse with Lina doubled up at his back; she was held in a trance and under his control. The evil one from down below, called the deceiver with many names, had spared Lina's life to use her for this very moment in time. It was true; Jack's dead wife's soul had been captured long ago by the devil and was now a part of Lina; all she had known was that the Preacher seemed familiar and she was attracted to him upon first sight. She was stronger than she knew; she housed her natural born soul along with the soul of another, the soul of the lost; in time if Lina could come to her understanding and faith she could be more powerful than any demon, but at this point she was easily controllable by the evil that held her.

The rain fell steady, and by mid-day it seemed as dark as twilight. While in their demon form the vampires had tried to feed upon the Navajo braves that they killed in the ravine but to no avail, for demons cannot feed on angels. Only the brave's horses had provided some nourishment. The army of evil needed blood for sustenance; they were like alcoholics gone too long between drinks. Andelko prayed to his evil master as he conjured up a spell changing the life giving rain water into life giving blood for his evil warriors. Their heads went straight back as they marched south, mouths open taking in the blood rain from the sky. Their necks were bent further than humanly possible and contorting in an unnatural way.

White Owl led the way, followed by Jack then Richard on their mounts, and then the remaining braves marching in a line at the rear. When the rain turned to blood Jack and Richard covered their nose and mouth with bandanas to keep the cursed liquid from entering. The chief and his braves protected themselves from the blood by their status; white wings grew from their backs and made a shield above their heads, coming together like a canopy of feathers. Jack had to back away as the Chief's wings appeared, the span of Owl wings were much larger than that of the braves. Jack turned to make eye contact with Richard while he said with excitement, muffled through the cloth that covered his mouth, "I knew it! He is the White Owl. You know what, Richard, my brother, I reckon we just might win this thing."

"Don't secure an abundance of enthusiasm, Preacher," warned Richard. "For as much power is the good, there is equal power that is the wicked."

"I reckon that's true, Colonel," Jack replied with a grin, "but we have one thing that our ancient enemies don't."

"And what would that be, Preacher?"

"Faith, my brother, we got faith."

Richard said nothing, but he did seriously think on it for a moment; and for the first time that he could ever remember hope crept into his being. Things were changing, he was changing, and he trusted it was for the better.

With a new confidence, Preacher Jack rode tall in the saddle, sipping his whiskey, and he was determined to destroy the evil and save his girl. They were outnumbered, he knew, but history showed that good always finds a way to triumph over evil as is written. Jack believed this; the question he kept asking himself—was he a prophet or a pawn? This was not Revelation like it was written in the Bible, this was something else. Satan, Devil, Beelzebub, the deceiver, the fallen angel with many names was making a move on humanity, one that the prophets of the past, Matthew, Mark, Luke and John, had not foreseen. In other words, Jack was improvising, following with his head but also with his heart, spirit and soul.

After what seemed like a long period of time, the blood rain turned clear suddenly and began cleansing the earth by washing away the red. The Chief's giant wings went straight out with a span of eight feet and then retracted at his back and disappeared. Jack looked behind him to see that the braves had also retracted their wings, turning to their original native form.

"Does that hurt, Chief?" Jack asked.

"Pain is for the sinners, Preacher. When the dwelling of God is with men and the old order of things has passed away, there will be no more death nor mourning nor crying nor pain."

"I will take that as a no?" Jack said with a grin, for the whiskey was kicking in, creating the liquid courage he would need to survive this day.

Hours passed and the rain had stopped but the purple and black clouds remained. The good army traveled on with little or no talk; the braves never spoke and the Chief always had to be persuaded to converse. Jack took the time to nap in the saddle for much needed rest while Richard just quietly stared ahead. Jack figured night was coming, but it was hard to tell the difference with the sun behind the ceiling of low hanging clouds. Blue lightning suddenly began to light up the sky three to five miles to the south in the direction they were headed. The flashes were spread out wide across the canyon at first and then they came together concentrating at one spot in the middle deep into a ravine. White Owl stopped as Jack and Richard came alongside.

"The Evil has found the entrance to the cavern where the God's laws are hidden," the chief said this with his normal emotionless tone. "They have followed the signs of the Knights Templar that have led them to this place."

The blue lightning was steady and bright flowing from the sky to the ground when it suddenly turned red from the ground upward and with a flash of white light it was gone. The trumpet sounds of the Ancient Israelites could be faintly heard riding on the wind throughout the land.

"What was that, Chief?" Jack asked.

"The door is open, the evil has entered."

"That's just great," said Jack, "we are too late then?"

"No," said the Chief, "they may enter but the Ark will defend itself."

"What do you mean it will defend itself?" Richard asked.

"Yes, it will," answered Jack, "I understand this, from Samuel II, and when they came to Nachon's threshing floor, Uzzah put forth his hand to the ark of God, and took hold of it; for the oxen shook it. And the anger of the Lord was kindled against Uzzah; and God smote him there for his error; and there he died by the Ark of God."

"This does sound reasonable Preacher," said Richard, "so no one can lay their hands upon the Ark or they will be struck down."

"No one but the chosen," White Owl said, as he turned and looked to Jack.

Jack smiled and laughed uncomfortably as he rubbed his forehead. "That's just great, there, Chief, I'm just gonna take your word for it and throw that Ark right on my back and carry it off?"

"If that is God's will."

"Your braves are angels not of this world—can they carry the gold box without sufferin' God's wrath?"

"Angels are forbidden to meddle into the affairs of men," the Chief said plainly.

"Oh, really," proclaimed Jack, "is that right, I seem to remember a time ago, I was minding my own business when you found me drunk in a shack in the middle of the desert and dragged me down this dangerous road."

Chief White Owl ignored Jack's speech, keeping his relentless pursuit of the mission at hand. "We must go, time is short."

Jack did not argue, even though he was extremely tired and a little liquored-up, so with no more talk they continued on with their chase.

Andelko Balas had followed the crosses and hooked X's carved into the rock by the Knights Templar thousands of years ago; he did this under the lightning filled sky. The vampire's keen sense told him where to scratch and chip away at the buildup of sand and mineral that covered such signs. When the writings were uncovered the crosses would glow blue for a second or two, clearly irritating Andelko. He was led down a corridor of rock at the base of a large mountain cliff and with his large hands he stuck his fingers with newly grown claws into the barely seen grooves that outlined a door. The old vampire ignored the blood that seeped from under his nails as he scraped the loose sand to uncover the opening. Andelko gave the rock slab a push with the force of ten men; to his dismay, nothing moved. He then spotted a marking covered in loose top sand where a door handle might be; after wiping it clean with his bloody fingers he found another, two sunk-in crosses appeared one on the left and one on the right and were carved into the center of two circles. Andelko put his fingers in the middle of the crosses and simultaneously turned the left to the right and the right to the left toward one another; with a loud click dusty smoke shot out from the seams of the outer rim of the ten foot high by six foot wide door as it sunk into the mountain. As soon as the door began to move all the lightning in the sky concentrated at that one spot. The blue sparks energized the entire ravine; Andelko could feel the power of the electricity trying to stop his human heart. He fought back with all his evil and feeling confident until the trumpets sound. His hands went to his ears, covering them, for he thought his head was going to explode. Suddenly a crack in the ground appeared behind him and the ground shook; with help from his master a red flash like lightning shot upward from the depths of the earth and collided with the blue from the sky and with a flash of white the air was suddenly calm and the sounds of the trumpets faded. Without a word from Andelko two of his Apache vampire warriors shot past him with Lina in their grasp. They released her and pushed on the slab of rock moving it into the mountain and stopping only when it hit against the back wall revealing a tunnel to the right with chiseled steps that led downward into the strange black darkness. Andelko took the right turn and then realized even he had trouble seeing in this blackness. To his left at the third step he could just see a torch mounted high on the wall; with a touch of his clawed finger it lit up in the color of red. Underneath the torch and carved in the rock wall were words written in ancient Pueblo: it read 'Cave of the Dogs'.

Every twenty steps there was a torch fastened to the wall; as they descended down the corridor Andelko lit each one as they went creating a bloody red glow to light their way. Lina walked obediently behind Andelko in his search for the Ark of the Covenant.

The army of good led by chief White Owl had shortened the distance between them and Andelko's demons, as they now stood in front of the entrance of the cavern several hours after Andelko had entered. Leaving their horses to graze topside they walked down the passage that was clear and lit by a red glow that made Jack feel slightly nauseated as they stood in the doorway.

"The torch light reeks of Andelko's power, it turns my stomach," said Jack as sweat ran down his brow.

"You would be correct, brother," said Richard, "and he is welcoming us to follow. I do not believe it would be in our best interest to do so."

"We will follow," said White Owl, "for the battle of this earth continues within these mountain walls."

"Well, let's git on with it, Chief, I'm right behind yah but watch yourself 'cause I might lose my stomach innards at any moment. This tunnel reeks."

"Ye of little faith, Preacher," White Owl said as he took the first three steps downward to the first torch. He touched the burning flame with his index finger and with a small flash of white the red turned to blue. The downward stairs were lit in a new light that was soothing, Jack's sickness immediately went away and his strength returned. Jack and Richard followed the old Indian down into the mountain with the six remaining braves bringing up the rear; every twenty steps they came upon a red glowing torch that White Owl changed to blue with a touch.

The narrow passage carved through the rock continued downward for a quarter mile to where the steps ended and the ground leveled out. Another hundred yards brought them to the last torch where the passage widened into darkness; White Owl reached up and made contact with the red glow which turned white and then blue once again like all the others. Jack came alongside the Chief, for he could feel the change in their surroundings. Richard came alongside

Jack, also feeling the change in the air, glad to be out of the restricted passageway. The blue light of the last torch jumped like slow moving lightning to another that was fastened to the rock wall of the big room, and then another, and another creating a semi-circle to their right and to their left, twenty feet from that torch it lit up another and continued on showing the rounded shape of the cave and turning the darkness into light. The blue light stopped with a flash; and twenty feet from this last blue torch, the next to follow lit up but in the nasty red color that was Andelko's.

The Indian chief, the preacher and the colonel walked out to their left from around the wall and followed the torches on the far side of the cave with their eyes as they lit up like before but in the evil color of red, lighting up the cavern that was the size of a medium lake sunk down in the mountain. The red fired torches were on the far side of the round room and the blue fired ones were on this half where they stood, a representation in color: good versus evil. Jack looked down now to the center of the large cavern to see what was twenty feet below; his heart sunk to see Lina tied to a wood cross with stacks of wood at her feet. Andelko was by her side and the Apache vampires stood spread out on their half of the cave on steps under the red glow of evil. Jack glanced backward as the six Navajo braves fanned out behind him and their Chief; they looked small in number compared to the Apache vampires. They all walked down the stone ramp in unison, bringing them closer to the center were the line was drawn with the red and blue light dividing the room. Andelko stood next to Lina tied upon her stake on the side of the red glow. Jack kept his eyes on her as they drew closer; she seemed to be in a daze looking straight ahead not aware of her surroundings or their presence.

Jack and Richard came to a halt by the Chief's side at the edge of the blue light. Andelko stood alone within reach of the stacks of wood piled under Lina's feet. Jack noticed the wood was very dry but the master vampire's head fused to the Apache chief's body did not hold a torch; the closest fire was high on the wall at his back and at his sides. This gave Jack some hope they might be given some time to reverse this bad situation.

The small army of good stood across from the large army of evil with a distance of twenty feet where the blue light and red light from the torches met on the ancient cave floor showing where the line was drawn.

Andelko was the first to speak. "Ah. The great White Owl, we finally meet face to face. I knew one day this time would come, for it is our destiny."

"Destiny?" said White Owl. "I think not, destiny is what must come from what is written. The fallen angel which dwells below has shown no patience. Your master of evil has forced us to meet, for we have free will to walk away and end all this, do you have the strength to do the same?"

Andelko's eyes turned brighter red with anger, for he knew there was no free will on the dark side: his power came with a great price. The eyes of the vampire Apache army also began to glow the red color and they began to hiss. The sound made Jack's spine grow cold; he looked to Richard and could tell he could feel this as well. Jack suddenly stepped forward, for he felt he must to keep the negotiations going; they were outnumbered greatly and cooler heads would prevail.

"What is it that you want with the girl, vampire?"

Yes, Preacher," said Andelko as his eyes calmed to normal stopping the hissing sound throughout the large room. "Look upon her faces and see what you will see."

Jack gazed at Lina; to his horror her face changed slightly showing his lost wife of long ago trapped within. "You evil bastard, what have you done?"

"It was not I, but the beast that stole her soul and merged it with this woman to assure you do as you are told. You cannot defeat me, Preacher."

"As I recollect, I was the one that took your head, vampire." Jack said this trying not to show the panic that dwelled up inside him.

"Yes but I live once again, there is no defeating the power of the beast."

"What is it you want, Andelko?" asked Jack and getting to the point, for this pointless measuring of their manhood was getting them nowhere fast.

"Yes, Preacher, let's get on with the business at hand," replied Andelko with the raising of his arm toward a large doorway in the cave wall. "In that doorway is the Ark with your God's laws contained inside; the White Owl's angels disguised as braves will transport it for me, at your orders of course."

"And if we don't?" asked Jack, as he slowly put his hand on the butt of his Colt.

"If you refuse to do so, Preacher, my army of demons will destroy you, but only after I light this lovely pile of wood into a glorious fire at the feet of your beloved."

Jack contemplated this warning. He glanced at Richard, who had one hand on the hilt of his sword, the other on his pistol butt. White Owl stood his ground with his usual calm expression. Jack continued,

"I doubt even with your great power you could summon a torch from the wall before I put a silver bullet through your forehead, you think?"

Andelko flashed an evil grin and raised his hand slowly, his bony clawed fingers leading the way; Jack tensed up, preparing to draw and fire, confident that he would not miss; he then loosened up with temporary defeat as Andelko's finger lit up with the evil red flame as he moved it down toward the pile of dry brushwood.

"Stop!" Jack exclaimed. "Ok, master vampire, you got power, I can see that."

Jack was angry at himself, for he should have known Andelko could light the fire with a touch, for the chief had done the same by his hand to light the torches.

Andelko smiled wide, showing his fangs in triumph, and then Jack continued the conversation with a challenge.

"If your evil power is so great, why don't you send your own demon warriors inside the cave to carry the golden box; or is that something you might fear?"

Andelko's expression changed for a moment as this challenge was put upon him. The fire at his hand extinguished as he stared down the preacher.

"I fear not, preacher man, so we shall see."

Without a spoken word, four Apache vampires crawled crab-like along the walls toward the cave entrance. Jack noticed that they avoided the line of the blue light that split the center of the doorway with the red light; he glanced to Richard and saw that he had also noticed their fear of the blue light.

The vampires went inside as commanded by Andelko. Moments passed in unnerving silence as the Chief, Jack, Richard and Andelko watched with anticipation. Lina continued to stare straight ahead in her trance, unaware of the goings on.

Suddenly there was a flash of white light that came from the rock doorway, followed by agonizing growls that turned to screams and then deep silence. The passage that had been split down the middle with the light of blue on one side and red light on the other was now totally blue giving more of the cave towards the good.

Andelko turned to the preacher to see a smile on his face for this small victory. Andelko spoke with a reluctant expression of anger.

"Well, as you can see, the angels of blue must carry the Ark, as I said from the beginning."

Jack crowded White Owl with his back to the master vampire.

"Well, it's your call, there, Chief, do we carry the box and travel with this evil or do we fight it out here?" Jack said quietly so that Andelko would not hear, but Richard knew that Andelko's hearing had no bounds in this room.

"I can tell you this, Preacher; here is not the place for the final battle." White Owl replied.

After a pause and a long stare with the chief, Jack mulled it over, and then walked with his head high right toward the Master Vampire; Richard's hand went to his sword as he tensed up. Jack stopped at the edge of the blue light, face to face with Andelko, who stood at the edge of the red light; neither one flinched in the slightest.

"Ok, vampire, we will carry the Ark for you but not until you release the Indian woman to me. If not we can throw down right here and right now, 'cause frankly I'd have no problem removing your head a second time."

Andelko showed a big and nasty grin, exposing his fangs; the smell that resonated from his breath disgusted Jack, it took all his strength not to take a step backward.

"Very well, Preacher, take the woman, but do not think that I cannot control her from a distance or end her life at any time that I wish by my will."

Andelko raised his clawed hand in the air; as he did so the ropes that held Lina to the cross fell away. The master vampire then waved his long fingers in a come forth motion; Lina somehow navigated the wood pile under foot and walked to Andelko's flank. Andelko backed away further to his side of the cavern and then released Lina from her trance. Her eyes blinked with sudden clarity looking into Jack's; she immediately went to him and hugged his chest with a sigh of relief. Jack walked her deeper onto the side of the blue light, as far away from Andelko as they could go.

Four Navajo braves made their way to the cavern were the Ark of the Covenant had incinerated Andelko's demons just a short time ago. Everyone watched with great anticipation as they entered; no flash ensued as before. After a time white light glowed from the cavern as the braves came forth with the Ark. The Navajo braves were two on each side of the gold-laden box; their wings were out and the blue light was radiating from them in a protective barrier. The Ark was two and a half cubits long, a cubit and a half wide, and a cubit and a half high. The overlay was of pure gold. There were four gold rings fastened to its sides two on each, where poles of acacia wood were inserted to carry the box. Two gold Cherubim with their wings spread upward and facing one another were hammered as one piece on the top of the cover.

Andelko backed away, trying not to show any distress; his army of Apache vampires could not contain their fear as they backed away deep on the side of the cave lit in red as far away from the Ark's white glow as they could reach. Andelko and his army would follow White Owl, the preacher and the Ark at a distance to their next destination, further south to the cave of the Knights Templar where Jack and Richard had first met up with White Owl and his army of Navajo warriors.

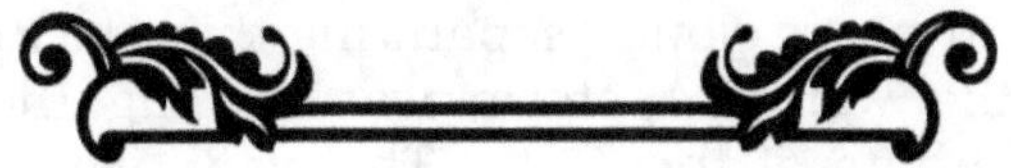

CHAPTER TWELVE

Exodus 23:20
*Behold, I send an angel before thee, to keep thee in
thy way, and to bring thee to the place
which I have prepared.*

The white wolf named Marchosias and his pack of black wolves had followed the Chief's army of angels knowing that they held the blue light of the father. They kept their distance and observed from afar until the good army had entered the hidden resting place of God's laws. They moved in closer to the entrance of the cave and waited to see if anyone would exit but staying quiet and out of their sight. Marchosias knew if the battle were to take place down inside the mountain he and his wolf brethren would possibly miss their opportunity to regain their status before God.

Marchosias and the four black wolves that followed him had made terrible mistakes in their lives long ago, falsehoods driven by greed and their hunger for power and status had been their Angelical undoing. The only way Marchosias could ever be Dantanian once again would be by the grace of the Father, the Son and the Holy Spirit. The white wolf could only hope that being on the good side of this holy war would return him and his brothers to their rightful status as angels to the throne of heaven.

Hours had passed; the wolves sat on the ledge far away but within the distance of their sight. The land over the canyon of grand was covered in low hanging purple and black clouds separating this place from the rest of the world. A storm was coming that would decide the fate of the earth. The white wolf's panting ceased and his ears went upward when he saw the white feathered head dress of the Chief appear from the crevasse. The chief of the Navajo was followed by the Preacher then the half-blood woman, then the soldier of Romania. Then there was blue light that preceded the appearance of the Navajo angels that carried the Ark of the Covenant in a melodic march and heading further south. Marchosias was surprised when he saw Andelko and his coven of demons following the good army; though they kept their distance they were clearly traveling together, this was not expected but it was good news for the wolves to carry out Marchosias' plan. Normally this would be the time for the white wolf to howl, followed by his pack to let their selves be known, but not at this time; they would shadow the vampires and follow until the time was right to reveal their status in this battle. The sky over the Grand Canyon was dark and the clouds were spinning slowly counter clockwise. The sun was blocked entirely and the wind swirled at a steady breeze. There was no rain or lightning, but the feeling in the air gave the impression that a storm could break out at any moment.

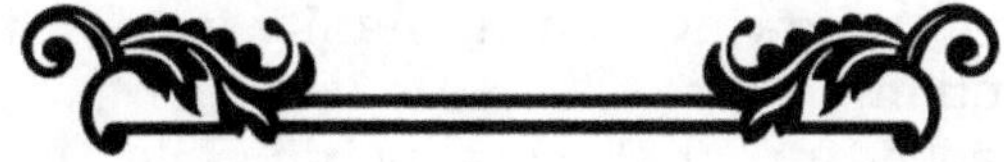

CHAPTER THIRTEEN

Matthew 26:64
*Jesus said to him, Thou hast said it; nevertheless I
say unto you, here after shall ye see the son of
man, sitting at the right hand of the power of
God, and come in the clouds of the heaven.*

The rest of the world went on as was usual outside the land of the canyon as humanity was oblivious to what was taking place here, good versus evil in the war for the control of the earth in this year 1886. On the outside of the canyon and across the rest of the country, history was being made as life went on, life that seemed important for those who were ignorant of what was taking place between heaven and hell.

The Democrats had regained the White House for the first time since the Civil War with President-elect Grover Cleveland.

A pharmacist invented a carbonated drink called Coca-Cola.

A hurricane hit Indianola, Texas.

An earthquake shook Charleston, South Carolina, leaving 40,000 homeless.

Five hundred miles from the battle taking place in the Grand Canyon, Geronimo surrendered with his last band of warriors in Skeleton Canyon, Arizona.

In this same year, 1886, President Grover Cleveland dedicated the statue of Liberty far away in the city of New York.

Men went on living their lives outside the Grand Canyon, not knowing that humanity was on the brink of destruction.

Jack looked up at the low swirling clouds from the back of his horse with a feeling of recollection as they rode single file.

"Them clouds look awful familiar, there, chief, like the ones over the Black Mesa Mountain not so long ago."

"Why would the clouds not be the same, preacher?" questioned the Chief, "we fight in the same war only not the same battle."

Colonel Richard broke in on the conversation. "I sense that Andelko is at his weakest around the Ark and the blue light; I brood over this, for right here and now could be the time for the last battle, this he would not expect."

"Good has always been stronger than evil," said Chief White Owl, "but their numbers are still too many and Holy ground is what we seek."

Lina spoke from her mount in line behind Jack and in front of Richard. "We are returning back to the cave of the Knights Templar, is this so?"

"How do you know of the cave of the Knights Templar?" asked Richard. "We found you in the river miles north, after our departure."

"I do not know how I know this, I just do," she replied with some confusion.

Richard considered she may still be under Andelko's power to some extent, he believed that Jack may not see this for he was blinded by her beauty and the soul of his lost wife that she kept. The Chief would most surely see the danger of Jack's weakness, but Richard could not read the old Indian and would not ask, for Richard was not sure if White Owl even trusted him as a foreigner born in the lands where the master vampire was created by the fallen-one.

Chief White Owl spoke as they rode their slow place.

"The caves of the Knights Templar is holy ground and was one of the many hidden spots of the Ark; it was meant to be the last, but some time ago the Navajo braves, with wings spread, moved the Ark at a time in the past for reasons that are not clear in my mind."

"Whoa up there, Chief," interrupted Jack, "you mean to tell me you and your army moved the box to where we just came from and now we are bringing it back to the tombs?"

"This is the truth. God's laws needed to be kept safe and the Knights slumber was not complete, they needed time to rest."

"Man oh man, "Jack said, "You're stories git better and better for sure."

"Preacher, you are not listening," said Richard, "White Owl said of the Knights in their slumber, not in their death."

Jack grinned as his mind became clear. "Yes, of course; the Knights can't protect the Ark if it is not in the tombs of the ancients."

"The number of Knights is six, that would be six more than we have now, if they wake—will they wake Chief?" asked Jack.

"If it be God's will, Preacher, it will be so."

Jack nodded in agreement. His eyes looked up to the sky. "I will pray for it, 'cause we sure could use the help as we are clearly outnumbered."

Richard said, "If they awake, Preacher, they will be fierce warriors, for they are from the Holy Land from a time of the beginning."

"I'm sure they will be just that, brother, I am sure." Jack said this with some confidence that he did not have moments ago.

The small army of good made their way south carrying the gold-laden Ark with Andelko's army of evil following at a comfortable distance, keeping away from the power of the blue and white light. The pace they traveled would bring them to the Tombs of the Ancients in one and one half days where Andelko would have to persuade the preacher to open the Ark and destroy the tablets within. His plan was to recapture Lina while his warriors fought with White Owl and the Navajo braves. Andelko knew that the preacher and Lina's love for each other was growing rapidly now that they knew Jack's dead wife's soul was a part of her. Andelko did not believe the preacher would sacrifice her again, not even for his miraculous God, for the preacher's faith was far from that of Abraham's, written from the book of Genesis, Abraham who did sacrifice his son for God only to keep his child at the last moment as the Holy Spirit directed the blade of Abraham's knife away from his son's flesh. Abraham passed the test of God; Andelko did not believe the preacher's faith was strong enough to pass the test, and the vampire's plan relied heavily on it.

Jack knew White Owl's plan was to reach the tombs of the Knights Templar, after that only God could know what would happen next. He kept looking back at Lina who rode quietly only smiling back when he smiled at her first. Her eyes were different and Jack could see that his long dead wife's soul lived on in this half-breed woman. Jack swore to himself then and there that he would protect her life this time, come hell or high water. Jack steered his stallion out of line and slowed to come alongside Lina. White Owl continued on and the Colonel slowed his pace, backing up the line of braves behind him and creating separation for allowing the Preacher and the women some privacy. Jack appreciated the distance and made a mental note to thank his brother.

"Who are you Lina? Can you tell me what you know?"

Lina made eye contact with the preacher and smiled; Jack could see that her eyes were different, but at the same time they looked very familiar.

"Maria?" asked Jack.

"I am Lina, but Maria is a part of me somehow, she is in here." Lina rested her open palm on her bosom as she said this and a tear ran down her cheek. "She has always been with me since her death, somehow, but she was at the same time separate; we are now one."

Jack was happy and sad and angry, all at the same time. He knew that the plague that killed his wife and child and an entire village long ago was the work of the Devil for the purpose of this war of good versus evil. Jack also knew that God allowed it to happen for the same purpose.

"My daughter, our daughter, is she...?"

"She has moved on and is by the Father's side living in peace like no one can imagine."

Jack welled up with joy as they rode in silence for a moment; to himself he thanked the Lord.

"Maria began to come forward slowly from deep within, when I first set eyes upon you Preacher."

"Please call me Jack." he insisted.

"Jack," she replied, "you know you must not sacrifice what you must do for my life, this is the fallen-one's trap."

"I understand," said Jack, but inside he knew the curse was already working—for his first thought was to find a way to save her and at the same time defeat the evil one.

Suddenly his thoughts were interrupted by sounds coming from far behind the army of braves that carried the Ark and in the area of where Andelko's army followed.

The white wolf and the four black wolves had flanked the rear of the vampire Apaches and mounted a daytime attack upon them; even though the sky seemed dark the sun was high in the heavens above the clouds, not allowing the day-walkers to change to their more powerful form and giving the wolves an advantage. The four blacks attacked from the flanks: two on one side and two on the other, and they were about thirty warriors deep, splitting the evil army in half and lunging at the rear while the white wolf ambushed at the hindmost. The vampire Apaches were at a disadvantage and were ripped apart by the wolves as they fought with canine fangs barred; the vampires were no match for the warrior angels in their cursed carnivore form. In a matter of minutes, the vampires were depleted by twenty as their souls flashed with the red light and vanished downward and their bodies turned to dust from which they had come. The vampires known as day-walkers were weaker than the traditional blood-suckers of old, as they gave up a portion of their power for the right to survive in the daylight.

The great white wolf had finished off the last of the vampires at the rear while the black wolves had destroyed the flanks forcing the rest of the Apache cold-ones to retreat to the front of the line. Their retreat was not from fear but by order, for out of the sky came Andelko with his sword in his right hand and in the left he held the same tomahawk that cut off the head of the Apache chief that was now his new body. The master vampire landed between the four black wolves at his sides; they moved in cautiously, growling viciously with their teeth bared and coming in closer while circling, the hair standing straight up at the nape of their necks.

Andelko wasted no time as he threw the tomahawk at a black to his right; the wolf ducked his head and dodged to the side. The steel blade missed by an inch. Andelko pulled his revolver and shot the wolf between the eyes; the beast yelped one time and then fell to the ground dead. The other wolves had closed the distance between them and the vampire; the lone wolf to Andelko's right took several strides and jumped in an attack. Andelko turned and swung his sword with the speed of a rattlesnake strike and removed the wolf's head in mid-air. Both head and body hit the ground at the vampire's feet. The two remaining blacks lunged at the master vampire's left flank, one, then immediately the other; Andelko swung the sword in a back-handed motion that cut the throat deep, killing the first wolf. This move left Andelko vulnerable for the last wolf's approach. Its teeth-filled mouth was agape aiming for the throat; with great speed Andelko dropped his sword and grabbed the black over and around the head and into a lock, and then slung the wolf up and over and into a body slam. With ten times the jaw strength of a lion, the vampire sunk his fangs in deep and ripped out the throat of the animal's form and devoured the warm blood that flowed freely. This blood was that of one of God's angels which gave the master vampire a burst of great energy, for Andelko's status allowed him to feed on all creatures of this world and many others.

Andelko released the lifeless carcass, which fell to the ground as he then stood from his kneeling position; the large white wolf was ten feet in front of him and let out a howl to the heavens. Andelko's smirk became an evil grin as the angel blood dripped from his fangs. He then witnessed the transformation of the white wolf occur before his eyes. The howl ended when the white wolf called Marchosios, stood on his hind legs as the white wings of the phoenix grew from his back and spread out in an impressive wing span. The wolf that he was vanished, as he then turned back into his a long-awaited form; the angel Dantanian now stood before Andelko with a sword in hand. He wore a crown of gold and was tall in stature. His muscular body was that of a Greek statue and his skin was the color of white chalk.

"Ah, Dantanian," said Andelko with a friendly demeanor, "I see you have found a world that will accept you, what a shame you lived like a dog for so long."

"Those days will soon be over, Andelko. for I am here to pay the father for my sins," said the angel named Dantanian.

"Dantanian, you are mistaken, my friend, the fallen-one has come to claim his rightful throne upon this earth." Andelko stretched his hands up and out at his sides as he said, "Join us, and I will see that you get a commission in my army as a Colonel, or a General perhaps?"

"Never again, demon will I place myself before others; for I have seen the error of my ways and I will gladly forfeit my soul to the one and only creator of the universe, the Father, the Son and the Holy Ghost."

"That, Dantanian, will be your undoing," said Andelko as he opened his palm and summoned his sword, which flew in the blink of an eye from the ground where it lay and into his clawed hand.

Jack could not wait any longer for the chief to give the order; he stopped the army's forward progress when the commotion from the rear had grown to an uproar and was too loud to ignore. The preacher turned his horse around and came alongside Colonel Richard, who was already turned and looking back. White Owl and Lina joined them as the braves came to a halt, looking forward and seemingly uncaring about what was happening behind them. Growls and snarls could be heard, along with battle cries of the vampires, and then followed by yelps of pain and then turning quiet just to start up again.

"The wolves, they are attacking," Jack said with urgency, "we must help them."

"No," said White Owl, "it is not our fight; they must prove their faith to their maker and find their place by the father's side or under his foot."

"It don't seem right, Chief," complained Jack.

"We must continue on, Preacher, to the Tombs of the Ancients, that is where our battle lies." The Chief turned his horse and moved on; his braves followed, leaving Jack, Richard and Lina to the side. As soldiers Jack and Richard felt helpless while their allies fought for their lives.

"It don't seem right, brother," said Jack once again.

"I understand, Preacher," replied Richard. "The rules of engagement in this war are unlike any other, it is hard to ignore what we have been trained to do in wars past. I am forced to swallow my pride as I look to the positive as the battle will lessen the numbers of our enemy."

"But at what cost, I wonder?" Jack replied with some regret.

"We must go with Chief White Owl, please, Preacher," Lina pleaded nervously as she saw the Ark getting closer to their position as the braves moved forward.

Richard and Lina turned and left Jack to gain their rightful place at the front of the line, for there was a sense of danger in the air as the braves carrying the gold box with the Cherubs on the top moved closer to their position. Richard and Lina felt death in the air that surrounded the Ark; Jack only felt a good and great power radiating from the golden box that seemed to call to him.

Jack had to force himself to move on, for a sudden flash of red and white light appeared high in the sky from where Andelko's army marched.

As soon as the hilt of the master vampire's sword reached his grasp, Andelko shot straight up into flight; Dantanian flew after him in an attack. In the dark sky their swords slashed, clanked and clashed, every point of contact was a death blow that lit up the sky with red and white light. Andelko's form had changed and his wings were dark and made of human skin with a span greater than the pure white feathered wings of Dantanian. They battled as if it were their last, spinning so violently that they created a cyclone of wind with lightning that flashed when their swords met. Dantanian suddenly did something that Andelko did not expect, when he moved forward into the calm of the tornado and, placing his sword straight up in front of his face and stopping in mid-air, he closed his eyes and kissed the silver. An evil grin came across Andelko's face as he arrogantly thought this angel was surrendering his life because of Andelko's great power. Without hesitation, the vampire struck with his sword laterally, intending to cut Dantanian in half. As soon as the red light from his steel followed through, the flash of white light was enormous, displacing the cyclone to nothing as the white angel vanished. The force knocked Andelko backwards and slammed him to the ground. Several vampire Apaches met their master and helped him to his feet; Andelko cursed when he realized he had been tricked. He had lost many warriors in the attack of the wolves and now he had released the angels of their canine curse to the heavens. Andelko watched as the black wolf carcasses changed into their natural bodies and followed Dartanian to the sky in their angelical form to take their rightful place by the Father's side.

Andelko had lost thirty-two demon warriors in this battle of deceit, and he was forced to fight off the distress that crept into his being, for his evil master would surely make him pay for this loss. Andelko took flight and summoned his depleted army to march back up to their safe distance behind the Ark and continue on to the Tombs where they would destroy God's laws and take this world once and for all.

Peals of thunder roared behind the lightning of the sky; the flashes were extreme and pained the eyes of Jack, Richard and Lina, even White Owl had to cover his face briefly while they all fought to control their horses from fleeing.

"It is done." White Owl said with authority. "The wolves have been redeemed, at the same time lessening the numbers of the evil army."

Jack made the sign of the cross on his chest; Richard copied the ritual awkwardly, feeling a little unworthy to do so. He hoped that this God was a forgiving God and would pardon him some for his slow ignorance.

They continued on; they were one day away from where the Knights of the Templar slumbered. Three hours from now night would fall and the good army would camp for a meal and rest. The remaining gargoyles of Andelko's army would feed with the coming of the night, warm blood is what they sought and Jack, Richard and Lina were the only edible flesh in their proximity. Andelko had the demons under his control, but the blood thirst that drove them must be quenched. Jack and Andelko where having the same thoughts at the same time, as both had similar dilemmas; Jack needed to live to serve the purpose of the Father and Andelko needed Lina to live for the purpose of controlling Jack to destroy the tablets that marked Gods laws.

A tent was set up in the valley for the Ark like that of the days of old and guarded by the angels of the Navajo braves. White Owl, Jack, Lina and Richard set up camp at the lead at a safe distance from the Ark. Andelko and his army set camp at the rear at an even greater distance from the golden box, for its power of good was very dangerous to the un-dead, as God's laws contained within the Ark were absolutely the opposite of what the fallen-one taught in his black church of deceit and destruction.

Lucifer, once a glorious and powerful angel in heaven, sought to be more powerful than God himself and as the last straw he refused to bow to the human creations called Adam and Eve, whereafter God cast him down to the bowels of the earth. Lucifer then vowed to destroy the human race which he blames for his fate. He blamed God and his son 'Jesus Christ', who had taken what the fallen-one considered as his rightful place by the right side of the Father in heaven.

Lucifer refuses to wait for the written time of Revelation, known as the rapture, for as it is written the Devil will fail; by changing the past during the now, the fallen one hopes to change the future where he will reign over the human race bringing hell on earth. The Devil's plan was clear to God, who knows all things, but for the angels and humans on the earth they could only follow their faith. Demons and vampires, took orders for they were pawns in a game with serious consequences.

The day had been barely lit under the black clouds that covered the sun, as the day turned to night and the stars and the moon were high above and covered in a blanket of cumulus gasses, the blackness of the night was somewhat unnerving for the living. Jack and Richard had built a huge bonfire for warmth and light, but the yellow flame only went so far and then it was swallowed up by the unusually thick darkness. White Owl sat smoking his pipe across from Jack; Lina sat close to Jack's right and Richard sat to Jack's left. They had finished a meal of venison stew that Lina had made and it was agreed by all that she would do the cooking from now on. Jack opened the last bottle of whiskey and took a long draw which immediately triggered an urge to smoke. He took another drink and then handed it to Lina; she took a sip and shook her head with a slight cough and quickly handed it back. Jack smiled and then handed it to Richard, who took it with a nod.

"We will reach the tombs tomorrow afternoon at best," said Jack, "I hope tonight will be a peaceful one."

"I do not share your easing, brother," said Richard, "the demons must eat tonight, and the last time I checked there is a shortage of warm blooded animals in these lands."

"Thanks for sharin' your negative thoughts, Colonel; I don't suppose you could let me relax for one minute?" Jack replied half-jokingly as he reached toward him for the bottle; Richard obliged.

Jack took a swig and then stared at the Chief for a time, watching the old Indian smoke his pipe in silence and stare straight ahead. *What a poker player the old Indian man would make,* thought Jack, except this wasn't a game and Jack needed answers.

"What do you say, there, Chief, have we come this far just to be eaten in our sleep by the demons?"

"It is true, Preacher," said the chief, "there is always danger in the night, but as the Lord provides for us he may also do this by providing for them."

Jack lit a cigarillo as he mulled this over,

"You always speak in riddles, Chief, that's what I love about yah. So I will accept that answer, for I'll bet that's the only one you're givin'. I reckon we will live to fight another day."

"Andelko is strong and has the demons under his control," continued the chief, ignoring Jack's tone, "but the demons have a weak life force and must feed often. We must sleep lightly and with caution."

Lina locked Jack's arm with hers and moved close to him; he welcomed this with a slight embarrassment but got over it quickly for Jack loved this woman that sheltered his long lost wife's soul inside her flesh. The preacher was glad when he glanced over to see that Richard had turned in for the night with his hat covering his face. The chief had stood and left his pipe burning at the fire and walked off into the darkness. Jack's first thought was to follow him; instead he and Lina lay down in each other's arms and managed sleep.

Jack did not know how many hours had passed when he was awakened suddenly; he was a little relieved to see that it was still night, for one more day of travel was all that separated them from the final battle at the Tombs of the Ancients. Lina and Richard were sleeping deeply and White Owl had not returned. Something in the darkness called to him; still fully dressed, armed with sword and his firearms, Jack stepped quickly out of the firelight and into the darkness in the direction where the Ark rested and then farther on to where Andelko and his army of demons should be. Jack was on high alert for he knew the demons must feed and they had not seen one track or any signs of wildlife in several days. Jack came to where the tent was pitched to hold the Ark. He stopped involuntarily; there were four five-foot-high torches stuck in the ground around the shelter as a protection from the darkness. There was a white glow coming from the Ark that could be seen inside the tent; after a short pause Jack gave it a wide berth and continued on, barely able to see three feet in front of his face. He came up on a slight ridge and there in front of him stood Chief White Owl. He was glowing in the same white light as that of the Ark, both his arms were raised to the sky, his wings were extended outward and his headdress began to flow with a cold breeze swirling overhead. The demon Apache vampires were in gargoyle form and swarming in the breeze above White Owl. Jack pulled his sword and stood at the ready. Suddenly, out of nowhere, down below the ridge a very large herd of big horned sheep appeared out of the night, there were forty in all. The flying demons dove down in an attack on the herd of rams. The chief backed away and retracted his wings; he then worked his way to where Jack lay in wait. The sound of a slaughter could be heard across the dark valley, it hurt Jack's ears clean down to his soul.

"Do not watch, do not listen," said the chief, as he hurried past. Jack followed quickly, as he was glad to get away from such a grueling scene.

Preacher Jack and Chief White Owl appeared out of the dark and into the firelight of the camp, which brought Lina and Richard to their feet, startled.

"What is it? Are we under attack?" Richard asked with his pistol drawn.

"No," replied Jack, "I think we might just make it through this night. The demons are feeding as we speak; it is a miracle of sorts."

Richard and Lina looked at one another with confusion.

"A herd of rams just happened by," Jack finished.

Lina came to Jack's side and hugged him tight and then released him as she sensed that he was slightly uncomfortable. Jack managed a smile.

"A herd of sheep, all rams, at night?" questioned Richard.

"Ask the chief, he was there first."

"The Lord has provided," said the chief as he returned to his pipe at the fire. He was joined by the rest as they tried to relax to catch what respite they could, for the coming of the next day was near.

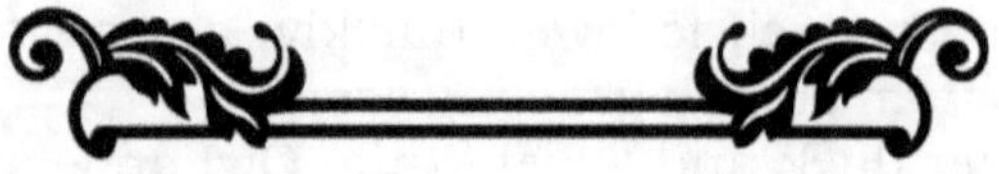

CHAPTER FOURTEEN

Proverbs 2:1-2:6
My son, if thou will receive my words, and hide my commandments within thee, And cause thine ears to hearken unto wisdom, and incline thine heart to understanding, For if thou callest after knowledge, and cryest for understanding, If thou seekest her as silver, and searchest for her as for treasures, Then shalt thou understand the fear of the Lord, and find the knowledge of God, For the Lord giveth wisdom, out of his mouth cometh knowledge and understanding.

The unusually dark blackness of the last night was gone with the coming of the morn, but the day was almost as dark as a normal night. The thick, low hanging clouds would not allow the sun's rays to penetrate and the sky was threatening to break into stormy weather at any moment. Jack traded his bed roll at Lina's side for the warmth of his duster as the wind was blowing steady and cool. He had awakened earlier than the others and struggled to heat the morning coffee on diminishing coals from the night's fire. Afterward Jack found a private place behind a rock; he set his knees upon the ground and prayed for guidance. He was satisfied that his prayer was worthy, but at the same time he felt disappointment for he needed an immediate response. He walked back the short distance to camp thinking to himself, *well what did you expect Jack, an answer, a one on one talk with God? It don't work that way and you know it, chosen one or not.*

Richard and Lina were sitting by the hot coals when Jack returned. Lina stood and handed him a tin cup of hot coffee, which he took with a smile and then squatted across from Richard. Lina joined them.

"Where is the White Owl?" Richard asked.

Jack pivoted on his heel and looked to where the Chief had bedded down just a few hours ago; there was nothing but his pipe leaning against a medium-sized stone.

"I reckon I don't know."

"Did you notice his presence when you walked off earlier?"

"I don't recall, brother," replied Jack, "but I thought so."

"He will return, yes?" Lina asked, clearly concerned.

"He always has in the past, after a while you get used to him disappearin' like he does."

"The clouds are in mass and sight is limited but I am sure it is the next day," said Richard, "the daytime is like the night, but it is more manageable than before."

"We are livin' in dark times, brother, but it won't be long now, the tombs are one day's ride from here at most."

"Preacher." From the dark a voice came that startled them; Jack turned on his heel and simultaneously pulled his revolver with great speed. Richard was at his feet with his pistols drawn. They both calmed when they saw who had approached.

"Where the heck have you been, Chief?" Jack asked as he stood and holstered his weapon. Richard did the same but stayed on alert.

"As you do, Preacher, I also hold my own council." White Owl replied.

"Ok, Chief, let's pretend I know what in the heck you're talkin' about."

To Jack's delight White Owl continued easily.

"I have returned from the Tombs of the Ancients, and from what I have seen the doorway is now blocked with rock."

"Can we unearth the rubble with our numbers?" asked Richard.

"The rocks are large; they are as if a doorway has never been there."

"That's just great," exclaimed Jack. "Well, maybe Andelko will just pack it in and we can all go home." Jack's voice dripped with sarcasm.

"Enlighten us, Chief White Owl, what must we do?" Richard asked.

"We continue on our path, the Spirit tells me the preacher will know what to do when we reach the Tombs of the Ancients."

"Great!" said Jack, "God speaks to you and then I gotta hear it second hand."

"He speaks to you, Preacher, but maybe you do not listen?" White Owl replied.

Jack stared at the old Indian with a bit of aggravation clearly on his face. A smart ass comment came to mind but he quickly bit his lip and reined in the thought before it escaped his mouth. "Ok, Chief, I guess I'll have to work on that, now let's git a move on. We have much work to do."

The small camp was struck in a very short time, and they headed out toward the cave in the darkness of the morning. White Owl led them with a lit torch in hand, Lina was behind the chief followed by Jack and then the Colonel; all were on horseback. There was a slight distance between them and the remaining Navajo warriors, the four which carried the Ark of the Covenant by the poles of wood and two which were holders of the torches. There was even a greater distance between the Ark and where Andelko sat upon his dragon horse and then the Apache vampires lined up and marching as one.

From a distance the firelight from the torches could be seen from White Owl at the front of the line to the last Vampire at the back, and stretched out for a mile; it was a sight to see for those to gaze upon it, but there were no witnesses to see what was happening here in the canyon of grand.

Jack was irritated for some time after the conversation with White Owl, but after a time he was deep in thought and focusing on scripture. The answer of how to clear the rock that blocked the cave entrance would be in the good book. In his mind he began turning pages, starting with Genesis; half way through the book of Deuteronomy something told him to relax, to clear his mind and the answer would come when needed. Jack suddenly stopped, his stallion halting the line at his back; he then spoke to Lina and Richard as White Owl continued on.

"Wait here, I must talk to the Chief."

"What is it, Jack?" Lina asked.

"I think I have found the answer to clear the doorway to the Tombs." Jack said as he rode forward to catch White Owl. Richard and Lina watched intently as the Preacher and the old Indian conversed up ahead. After Jack spoke they could see the Chief shake his head in agreement, and then he continued moving forward. Richard turned his body on top of his Clydesdale to see the two Navajo braves, which followed behind the Ark, leave and run off, back in the direction from which they came. The light of the torches that the braves carried became smaller as their distance grew. Jack returned to Richard and Lina's side. They both noticed that he seemed a bit more confident than he had all morning.

"We should reach the Tombs in about three hours." announced Jack.

"What is the purpose of allowing two soldiers to desert their post at the side of the Ark?" the Colonel asked.

"They return to the slaughter of the rams to retrieve some items," replied Jack, "I can't explain it right now but I promise brother, if it works it will be miraculous. The chief assured me that they will return."

Jack turned the black stallion and spurred the horse catching up to the Chief, the others followed close behind.

The two Navajo warriors ran hard, giving Andelko's army a wide berth, but they did not do so unseen. Andelko halted his dragon horse and watched the Navajo far off in the dark with the torch lighting their way. Andelko's first reaction was to slay the enemy by his hand but he then decided against it, for he was curious to see what the preacher and the White Owl were undertaking. He would allow the Navajo's desertion but he did send two of the Apache vampires to follow and observe what the angel warriors were doing. Soon they would reach their destination where Andelko had no doubt that he would destroy the preacher and take his rightful place by the evil master's side as a general in his great army. The fallen angel would be released upon this earth with many demons and rule hell from top side, one step closer to ruling the world and then the Heavens.

CHAPTER FIFTEEN

Joshua 5: 13
*Now when Joshua was near Jericho, he lift up his eyes
and looked; and behold, there stood a man against
him, having a sword drawn in his hand; and
Joshua went unto him, and said unto him,
art thou on our side, or on our adversaries?*

The army of good and the Ark of the Covenant arrived at the entrance of the Tombs of the Ancients in the mid-afternoon. The corridor to the door-way was completely filled with rock, many boulders too large to move as White Owl had reported. They would camp top-side of the blocked doorway, for the night was only hours away. Day was as dark as night but the night was pitch black as the low blanket of clouds still blocked the light that the moon and stars provided. White Owl sent two warriors to collect wood for a fire and the Ark was tented some distance away but within their sight. Four Navajo stood like guards outside the tent with the four torches that were lit on the four corners of the shelter.

Up above on the flat, and atop a small ridge, Andelko and his army camped within site of the good army but kept their distance from the Ark. The gold-laden box with the Cherubs on top had grown stronger and more violent energies could be felt by the cold-ones. Andelko did not want to lose any more demon warriors to the Ark as he had in the Cave of the Dogs.

The Navajo had returned with enough wood to last the night; the logs were dragged behind them on a flat of animal hide, where they then returned to the Ark. The fire was built by Jack and Richard and burning bright, a pot of coffee was resting on flattened coals at the side. They thanked God with a short prayer by Jack for the meal that they were about to receive, Lina had cooked salted meat that was on the verge of spoiling, it was roasted on a spit over the flames. Jack spoke as he finished the last bite of his meat.

"I have been goin' over it in my mind for some time now, and if you all will bear with me I think I have a fix." Jack got to his feet and walked over to his rig that had been removed from the stallion's back and was now resting on the ground; he returned with his Bible and sat down at his spot in the dirt and turned sideways to catch the light. He shuffled through the pages and stopped at the book of Joshua, and began to speak aloud.

"In a time long ago there was a great warrior named Joshua who was anointed by God to conquer the land of Israel as was promised to them; and at this time the Jewish people were the keepers of the Ark of the Covenant." Jack stopped his summary and looked up from the pages to see all his friends listening intently from around the fire. "There was a great city called Jericho that was surrounded by a great wall of stone and with the Ark they marched around it blowing horns loudly and then with a loud shout the walls of the city crumbled."

"So you say, Preacher," said Richard, "if we march with the Ark and blow horns and shout, the rock that blocks the entry will fall away?"

"Yes, Richard, that is the way in, the only way to remove the rock, I am sure of it."

"We have the Ark and we can shout but I do not believe we possess any horns to blow." As soon as Richard completed his question he realized the answer.

"The herd from the last night's slaughter, of course, the Navajo will return by morning with the horns of the rams!"

Jack nodded toward Richard with a grin, for he was pleased that Richard understood and more so that he believed.

"Andelko's impatience is well-known and he will wonder why we delay," Richard stated. "I shall make contact and inform him of the situation and of the dilemma at hand."

"You must not," said Lina, "he will kill you."

"I must," insisted Richard, "our gathering is way past due."

Jack did not like it any more than did Lina but he nodded in agreement.

"I will help you saddle up," Jack offered.

"No thank you, my brother, I will travel on foot for I will not subject my horse to such horrors," said Richard.

The temperature dropped suddenly as night fell to pitch black, only the fire light saved them from blindness. The chief was pointing off into the darkness toward the ridge where Andelko stood within—in a glow of his evil red light a short distance from their camp. Richard took a deep breath and grabbed a torch and touched it to the fire before walking fully armed toward his former master.

Lina was standing by Jack's side, her arm holding his as they watched the lit torch break through the night and move toward the red glow of Andelko, who had moved from the ridge and was now only fifty yards from their camp. Only White Owl had seen Andelko travel toward them and close the distance in the blink of an eye.

"I don't like it, Chief," Jack said with concern as he saw the red outline of the master vampire now only a short distance away, "he knew Richard was coming, he sensed it somehow."

"We must confront our demons, Preacher; we must confront them always alone."

Jack left Lina with White Owl and returned with his Yellow Boy rifle; he cocked the lever action, loading a bullet of silver in the chamber. He then pulled his sword from the sheath at his back and stuck the point into the ground; it resembled a cross marking a grave.

"I tell you what, there, chief, if he harms one hair on my brother's head I am gonna' unload this here rifle into his blood suckin' forehead." Jack said this as he got to one knee and rested the Winchester across the hilt of the sword and aimed it high at the base of Andelko's hair line.

Andelko and Richard were meeting for the first time since Richard had betrayed his master on the top of the Black Mesa Mountain, by running a sword through his back and piercing his dead heart. Like salting an open wound, Richard was now allied with Andelko's enemies, which was cause for much concern. Richards's safety was in grave danger, for he did not have the power of the vampire blood that he once had, from the bloodletting he was aging like any other man. He would have to rely on a new-found strength that was growing within him served by the God of heaven; his faith was still weak but strong enough that he did not fear death any longer.

Richard now stood face to face with the master vampire just out of sword's reach; Richard avoided staring directly into Andelko's eyes but still maintained a prideful stance with his head held high. Andelko was the first to speak.

"Richard, my old friend, why have you betrayed me so after all I have done for you?"

"After all you have done for me?" Richard replied sarcastically. "You corrupted my soul for over a hundred years and turned me into something that does not belong on this earth."

"That is where you are wrong my friend, the fallen-one will rule this world before the written time and I will be by his side in all his glory." Andelko said this with a raised prideful voice.

"There are some that would disagree with you, I being one of them." Richard replied.

"It is not too late for you, Richard; you can rule by my side as my number one once again while we crush the good army and enslave the human race for a thousand years."

"I think not," said Richard, "the God of the universe will prevail, if we all die in the process it matters not."

Andelko began to pace as his anger grew; unbeknown to him Jack had a rifle bead on the master vampire's head and was following him back and forth as he walked.

"You reek of human blood," growled Andelko, "you are weak…"

Andelko suddenly stopped pacing and glared over Richard's shoulder for a split second as if he sensed something and then he continued, "Maybe you need to be reminded who the master is here." With a blur Andelko lunged before Richard could react; Jack saw what was happening and pulled the rifle's trigger; the bullet of silver did not reach its target, for out of the darkness came a flying gargoyle, it exploded in a blue flash. Jack cocked the lever and fired again aiming for Andelko's head that was now next to Richard's as he bit down on his neck, another flying demon exploded in the blue light as it flew into the bullet's path.

"Nooooooo!" yelled Jack as he got to his feet. He intended to run to Richards's aid, but he was easily stopped by one hand upon his arm. The strength of White Owl's grasp was surprising.

"No, Preacher, you must not." said the chief.

Jack looked at the old Indian with desperation and confusion.

"Dammit, Chief, I can't leave him out there all alone!"

"He is not alone," The chief said plainly.

Jack looked back in the direction of their position to see nothing but darkness; the torch light that Richard held and the red glow that surrounded Andelko was gone.

"You must pick your battles, Preacher, the demons control the night and there are still too many. Andelko needs you alive for the moment but his control over the demon's blood hunger only goes so far."

Jack was pacing and glancing into the dark, looking for any sign of Richard.

"I got yah Chief, but as soon as the morn comes I'm goin' out there and I'm gonna find my brother. Andelko has broken the truce and I'm gonna kill him once and for all."

Lina walked up and wrapped her arms around Jack, stopping his pacing, for she feared he would dart uncontrollably out into the night.

"Please listen to White Owl," pleaded Lina, "Andelko plays on your emotion and he lays a trap for you in the desert."

She turned him and forced him to look into her eyes, "I have already lost my entire family and I will not lose you too."

Jack calmed as he looked into her green emerald eyes—he saw a glimmer of the soul of his lost love from long ago mingled with this beautiful girl before him. He looked out into the pitch black desert for any signs of Richard one last time before he joined White Owl at the fire. They would not sleep the last three hours of the dark, instead they would discuss the plan to collapse the wall of rock that blocked the entrance to the Tombs, and the answer lay in the Book of Joshua as he read in the Old Testament of his Bible.

CHAPTER SIXTEEN

Matthew 4:8, 9
*Again the Devil took him up into an exceeding high
mountain, and showed him all the kingdoms of the
world, and the glory of him. And said to him, all these
will I give thee, if thou will fall down, and worship me.*

They had not seen the sun for a week now and the
only way they knew the day time had come was they
could see more than an arm's length in front of their
faces. Jack had saddled his stallion and checked his
reloads before mounting. Lina handed him a lit torch
and smiled half-heartedly, "You be careful, Preacher,
find your brother and bring yourself back here to me."

"I'll do my best, little lady," said Jack with a smile of
his own before turning his attention to White Owl who
was standing by the fire. He reminded Jack of a
wooden Indian statue out in front of a town smoke
shop. Jack spoke to White Owl from the back of his
horse.

"As soon as your braves return with the horns of the
ram, begin the march with the Ark around the
mountain, seven times. I will be back before then with
or without Richard."

"Go with God, Preacher and all will be well."

Without another word Jack spurred the stallion to a
canter and headed straight out into the desert to
where he had last saw Richard. It did not take long for
him to reach the site of the battle, only fifty yards off.

The first sign that he came across of last night's action were two dead Apache vampire bodies lying on the ground; they had turned back from their gargoyle form with the coming of their death. They laid in wait for the sun rays to come and burn them to dust.

There were no signs of Andelko, but there was one set of staggered boot prints that trailed off to the west. Relieved that his brother was still alive Jack began to track from the back of his horse; it was sandy here in this part of the canyon, enabling him to move quickly as the boot patterns were deep.

An hour had passed; the stride of the foot prints had stabled and lengthened, telling Jack that Richard was strengthening, but why was he moving in this direction? He was abandoning his post, deserting the battle field. Retreat was not in this man's nature, and Jack knew this.

The terrain began to change as great rocks jutted up and out from the ground, creating hiding spots behind and around like a stone forest. The tracks were getting much harder to see, which was slowing down Jacks pursuit and he had no choice but to dismount and continue on foot. He held the reins and led his horse in tow. He then discovered he had a new type of trail to follow; it was drops of blood, the same blood of the vampire that had turned a desert scorpion into something wicked. *He's bloodletting,* thought Jack. He squeezed through rock formations barley large enough for the stallion to enter when he saw the colonel face-down on the ground and covered in a pool of the thick dark blood. Jack rolled him over to see that both his wrists were slit. Jack pulled a bandana from his pocket and ripped it in half; he used them to wrap tight Richard's wounds to slow down the blood flow while then checking his pulse at the neck. Richard was still alive but weak. Jack picked him up and leaned him against a wall of rock and then left him to retrieve his canteen from the stallion's saddle. On his return

Richard's eyes opened and he reached out for the water.

"Thank you, brother," he said, barely aloud, through parched lips. He took little sips, clearing his dry throat and allowing his voice to return.

"Saving my life is becoming a habit with you, Preacher."

"Lucky for you I'm a man of the cloth, it's my job to save," Jack replied with a small grin. "What the hell happened out there, brother?"

"Andelko could have easily ended my life; instead he decided to turn me, giving me an existence that I now loathe, an existence worse than death."

"Your blood is thinner Richard, and your eyes are clearing, the bloodletting has stopped the change."

"Someone saved me, Jack; there was a flash of white light and Andelko was thrown from me, all I saw were white wings like that of a bird for a moment. I lost time directly afterwards, not until I was on the move and bloodletting did I remember."

"The Chief said that you weren't alone out there, the White Owl was right once again, for this I am thankful. Now let's head on back for we have much work to do." Jack helped the colonel to his feet; blood dripped from the soaked rags at Richards wrists.

"I'm gonna have to seal those up," said Jack as he pulled a revolver from his holster. Richard nodded as he leaned back against the rock and pulled the ties off from around his wrists. Jack quickly fired two shots into the ground and then immediately laid the hot barrel across the cut on one wrist; Richard growled at the preacher as he shot two more shots and then again laid the heated steel against the other gash, scarring the wrist and sealing the skin from leaking.

"Damn you, Preacher!" exclaimed Richard. Jack had to grab Richard's shirt at the chest to hold him up, for his knees buckled for an instant.

"Can you walk out of here, soldier? We got a long day ahead."

"I have worse scars than this. Preacher, you lead the way and I will follow."

They maneuvered out of the rock on foot and then doubled up on the back of the stallion. When they reached the open terrain and rode back toward the tombs, they suddenly heard echoing off of the walls of the canyon of grand. They were sounds of horns that could be heard blowing across the wind.

The sounds of the trumpet became louder as Jack and Richard got closer to the tombs of the Ancients and then the blasts began to fade. Jack pulled back on the reins, bringing his black horse to a halt; he pulled out his scope and drew it to its full length and with one eye he aimed it in the direction of the fading sound. He saw the four braves marching with the Ark held up by the poles of wood and resting on their shoulders. With their free hands they were blowing the ram's horns they had retrieved from the feeding massacre two nights earlier. Two Navajo walked behind the Ark, blowing their horns and holding torches. Jack handed the telescope over his shoulder back to Richard, who took it and set his sights in the sound of the fading trumpets. Jack spoke while Richard looked on.

"They will circle the mountain seven times blowing the hollowed out horns of the Ram, and at the last round they will stop in front of the blocked doorway and then we will shout until the wall of rock crumbles to the ground."

"And you are certain this ritual will work to clear the stone?" Richard asked.

"It worked for Joshua, but he had many men and many horns. In the beginning the Ark had parted the river of Jordan in its flood stage in the season of the harvest, and the flow of the river upstream stopped flowing and it piled up in a heap allowing the Israelites to pass. They reached Jericho and encircled it with the Ark, the horns and the shouts from their army brought down the walls allowing them to take the city."

Richard handed the scope back to Jack. "They turned the corner of the mountain and dropped from my sight. When you speak from God's book your pronunciation, is different preacher."

"I was speaking from memory, and yes the good book was written in a time when language was much different than what we speak today. More like the speech from your land, my brother."

"I hope you will not change the way you speak, for I enjoy the accent. It seems welcoming somehow."

"Oh, don't you fret over that colonel; I reckon' my southern roots grow too deep. We best git movin'now before dad gits to worrin'."

They both smiled for a moment. The thought of Chief White Owl as their daddy was an inside joke between brothers. Jack spurred the stallion back toward the camp; they secretly relished this moment, for where they were headed this may be the last time that joy would ever cross their path.

Jack and Richard made it back to where White Owl and Lina waited for their return. They had struck the temporary camp and were prepared for the short move to the doorway of the Tombs. The Ark had made its second pass around the small mountain and the horns could still be heard fading as they turned the corner for the third time coming. It took the Angelic Navajo braves forty minutes to encircle the hollow mountain, and on every turn the black clouds followed with them. The counter-clockwise motion of the clouds reminded Jack of the storm over the Black Mesa mountain top where he had decapitated the master vampire just over a year ago. The wind was picking up and heat lightning was flashing in the low hanging clouds and Jack hoped the storm would not produce rain, at least not until they could enter the tombs.

They all secured their horses while the Ark passed by for the fourth time between them and the mountain. The constant blast of the rams' horns became a bit louder on every pass and Jack had to speak up to be heard.

"How many is that, Chief?"

"The number will be four, Preacher." White Owl replied, seeming to speak louder somehow without raising his voice.

After the fifth pass Richard got Jack's attention by tapping him on the shoulder and then pointing in the direction at his back. Jack turned and looked toward the top of the ridge where he could see Andelko and his vampire warriors lined up on foot and lying in wait.

"What has happened to Andelko's dragon beast?" Jack asked Richard.

"I could not say." Richard replied.

That is some sloppy military battle tactics, demon, thought Jack, as he was able to count their numbers, for they were two feet apart from one another in a line and in clear view. Proud Plains Indians of all tribes often did this to show their numbers, but in this case it was not to their advantage to do so—Andelko was once again showing his arrogance. There were now thirty-eight Apache vampires and Andelko; against the six Navajo warriors braves plus three and Lina, the odds were getting better and better for the good army but there were still many unknown forces involved here. Jack suddenly had the urge to pray when the horns blasted as the Ark came around the corner of the rock wall to pass for the sixth time. The blasts of the horns were louder and the storm was growing stronger as White Owls braves made their last pass with the Ark.

The blasts of the trumpets coming from the hollowed out horns of the rams did not fade on this last trip around the small mountain, and when they came into sight of White Owl and Jack the two men began to shout, followed by Lina and then Colonel Richard. The storm overhead intensified and the wind blew in all directions as the horns and shouts grew louder; blue heat lightning flashed constantly now until the braves stopped one hundred feet in front of the blocked doorway, still blowing on the horns continuously. All the lightning suddenly came together and struck down from the sky and hit the Ark between the Cherubs, the bolts of light shot straight across onto the mountain at the blocked entrance of the Tombs of the Knights Templar in an explosion that shook the earth. Jack, Lina and Richard took to duck and cover, the braves and White Owl did not flinch as rock fragments flew everywhere but somehow missed them all and flew past. When the dust cleared there was a large hole in the side of the mountain twice the size of the original doorway. The storm had calmed and the energy that was felt in the air had subsided, the clouds were still dark and swirling, but the lightning was dim and not as intense but spread out like heat lightning seen from a distance which helped the visibility of the gloomy day.

"My God!" exclaimed Richard. "That was an outstanding display of power."

"Yes sir," replied Jack, "men are strange, brother, when they see a miracle with their own eyes their faith is strong but time passes and they soon forget. The trick is to remember with the heart and the soul and spirit, and not just the mind."

"My faith is building preacher, with the God whom you call the father; I will not soon forget what I have witnessed here today."

Jack glanced up at the ridge top to see that Andelko and his army were gone from sight. "We best git a move on, and I would think Andelko is on his way down. Should we send the Ark in first, Chief?"

"We enter first; keep the Ark between us and the demons of the fallen-one."

"Yup, ok, chief that makes sense," agreed Jack. "The door is big now; we will walk the horses in with us. I ain't gonna leave them out here to become a meal for those Godless heathens."

They led their horses down into the tombs through the large opening, followed by the Navajo carrying the Ark of the Covenant; the six warrior angels followed them, still holding the ram's horns that were now silent.

Jack, Lina and Richard noticed immediately as they entered the tombs that the lightning strikes had done more than clear their path of fallen stone in the doorway; it had also sheared the top of the mountain completely off. White Owl did not have to peer upward to see what had happened here. The roof and ceiling were gone, revealing the sky of swirling blackish, purple clouds. They made their way down to the bottom of the large room that looked more like a Roman coliseum than a cave, especially now with its open rooftop .

As if summoned, the two Navajo braves that carried the torches appeared and took the horses' reins and led them away farther back into the cave.

"Where are they taking our rides, Chief? Jack asked.

"The animals will spook in the presence of the demons, there is a room place behind a rock wall that will shield them and beyond that there are narrow caverns leading to the outside if we must flee."

"I like the idea of having a back door to this place if things go south, but how do you know of these caverns, Chief? I don't recall you mentionin' this passage before." Jack said while crossing his arms.

"You have to be an Indian to know these things." White Owl said as he turned and walked away.

"I think he is says this in jest, Preacher?" proclaimed Richard.

"Oh, yeah, he's a laugh a minute, this one."

Richard clearly heard the sarcasm in Jack's voice, which forced a grin from the Colonel.

Jack continued, "If we live through this deal we can put the chief in the travelin' shows with Wild Bill Hickok, I suppose."

"Who is this Wild Bill you speak of?" Richard asked.

"I'll explain later, come on we best follow before Pa gets in a tizzy."

White Owl led them past the raised flat rock that had been erected in the middle of the floor and then across to the other side where they ascended upward using steps carved in the stone; some steps were natural and others seemed to be manmade, the first Masons from long ago were responsible for the inner carvings of the structure. White Owl settled on a large flat spot where the four could stand at arm's length between them and look down to the center of the huge space that made up the ground level.

The four braves that carried the gold-laden box had made their way to the center floor. They set the Ark onto the raised flat rock displaying the Cherubs standing proud on its top. The braves left it to stand on its own and joined their chief and the others, lining up at their back on the spot where they stood. The last two braves joined their brethren after securing the horses. There they stood, the small but gallant army of good waiting for the evil-ones that would surely come. Directly behind and high above them stood the Knights Templar, frozen in time. Looking down upon them and fossilized in their tombs like statues from the past. Jack turned his head and looked at the Knights almost expecting movement, but there was none. The cave was dimly lit as sunlight illuminated faintly behind the thick dark clouds from the peak that was now missing from the top of the mountain. Jack glanced up at the torches high above and wished they were lit; just as this thought crossed his mind Chief White Owl raised one hand and waved it around the room from torch to torch where they lit up with blue flame, making the room eerily brighter. Only their half of the cave was lit, the torches high on the walls of the other side where they had entered were dormant.

Andelko and his vampire Apaches had shadowed the Ark from a distance; after a time they crossed the threshold of the entrance that led down into the rock cave. Andelko could feel the power of the Ark growing inside the walls of the mountain.

Jack was about to ask White Owl a question when suddenly the un-lit torches at the entrance side of the cave came alive one at a time with the blood red light, revealing Andelko Balas standing with his arm outstretched. The red light canceled out some of the brilliance of the blue light; a symbolic energy good versus evil. Andelko's Apache vampires lined up behind their master along the ramp and upon the tiers of the steps and under the red light of their side of the cave that now suddenly looked to Jack more even more like the battle coliseums of ancient Rome. Only minutes had passed, but to Jack it seemed like hours as they all stood in dead silence fifty yards from one another.

"What's the plan, Chief?" asked Jack quietly from the corner of his mouth, not taking his eyes off Andelko and his warriors as he watched across the chamber for any movement.

Before White Owl could speak, Andelko answered the question loudly from across the coliseum of stone.

"There will be no plan, Preacher," said Andelko. His amplified voice reverberated off the rock walls. "A plan would suggest a plot of some sort, redemption is what I seek."

"You mean Revelation, ain't that right, demon?" Jack challenged, raising his voice to be heard.

"Call it what you will, Preacher, but the time of the fallen-one will be here and now."

"Only God can decide when the devil will be released on this earth, and now is not the written time." Jack pulled his Bible out from his belt at the small of his back and held it high, "maybe you should read it for yourself, here, would you like to gaze upon mine?"

Andelko scoffed loudly at the thought of touching the good book; it surely repulsed him.

"You will open the golden box and remove the tablets inside and crush them at your feet," demanded Andelko as he pulled his sword and pointed it down at the center of the room at the Ark that sat quietly upon its mount.

"Now why In God's green earth would I do such a thing?"

Before Jack could react Lina was suddenly at the edge of the flat where they stood some twenty feet above the cave floor; he should have seen her walk to the rim as she had been only three feet away from his side.

"Lina, no!"

Andelko slung his sword like a pointer from her to the Ark; she flew through the air as if catapulted and landed hard on the floor at the base of the raised rock that held the Ark. Her head hit hard and her neck whipped violently. Jack's heart sank and his panic turned to anger; the cross that hung from his neck began to glow blue and then traveled up his arm and into his sword as he pulled it from the sheath at his back. Jack began a run around the rim on the steps in an attack; Andelko flew through the air to meet him at the point where the red and blue light of the torches met at the side. The Apache vampires hissed and pulled their tomahawks, dropping down several tiers as they began a run to the line where the cave was divided by the multiple colored torches of light. The Navajo met them there with the horns of the rams as their weapons; they clashed as the fight was on. There were battles on both sides of the cave; the six Navajo soldiers were greatly outnumbered against the vampires; Richard had followed them to the far side, opposite from where Jack and Andelko battled. White Owl was the last to move and he went to Lina at the center of the chamber floor where she lay at the bottom of the cave at the base of the Ark.

The storm up above had begun to churn as the battle had begun. Lightning flashed and peals of thunder could be heard echoing throughout the canyon. An eye began to form in the center and four blood moons appeared across the sky, bringing on the night. The angels had the upper hand at the moment as the horns held power and slashed open the vampire's skin. The slashes they made, if not deep enough, healed quickly, but the same healing was possible for the angels when the tomahawks cut their flesh; at this moment the Navajo were holding their own even though they were outnumbered.

The blue and red light flashed where ever their swords made contact as Jack and Andelko thrust and slashed at one another. Andelko made a move that caught Jack off balance and the tip of the vampire's sword caught his hilt and separated Jack's sword from his grasped; Jack saw his silver blade soar behind him and to the left. Jack rolled forward, losing his hat, just as Andelko thrust down with his blade and just missed Jack's head by a hair. The preacher came out of his roll onto one knee and pulled a pistol, his left hand came down on the hammer as he unloaded six silver bullets, aiming for the center mass of the master vampire. Andelko shook violently as holes opened up in his chest and stomach. Jack holstered the Colt and went for his sword; he reached it and turned, expecting an attack from behind, but Andelko was not there. Jack glanced up and noticed the change in the storm for the first time; it looked similar to the gale that he had witnessed at the battle on the top of the Black Mesa Mountain one year ago, except there was something different that he found significant—the four blood moons that filled the eye of the cyclone.

Oh God no, thought Jack, *the night comes marked by the blood of the moons.*

The preacher looked down and across the chamber to witness the Apache vampires beginning to turn into their gargoyle demon forms as the night fell. Their skin covered wings formed, their three inch claws and fanged teeth dripped with a nasty fluid. The six Navajo changed quickly as their feathered wings protruded from their backs, the rams' horns turned to silver, increasing their power. The fighting took to the air as the demons and angels battled swirling and darting about, striking with spiked claws and the horns of the rams—the sounds of battle echoed loudly through-out the chamber.

Thoughts of Lina came to Jack's mind and he searched the ground floor with his eyes looking between and around the battling soldiers; through the chaos he spotted her now, leaning against the rock that held the Ark. Beside her, Andelko and White Owl engaged in a vicious battle of their own.

Don't kill him, Chief, for he's mine. Jack thought as he made his way quickly down the steps. He did not make it far before he was attacked by a flying demon swooping down with talons stretched and fangs barred; Jack turned and with one swipe of the sword of silver he took both clawed hands and the head in a flash of blue light. Another gargoyle was coming straight at him, flying from a distance; its screeching hiss alerted Jack to his frontal assault. Jack pulled the left handed Colt, cocked the hammer with his thumb and aimed for the forehead; with a pull of the trigger the loud boom of the powder igniting echoed as the demon's head exploded. Jack spun his body to the side as the carcass slammed the floor and slid by him, almost taking out his legs.

Jack took a deep breath as he tried to collect his bearings. He spotted Richard across the other side of the cave fighting with vicious swings of his sword at the top of the steps alongside the Navajo; the speed of the fighting was quick and intense as Jack witnessed two angels go down and vanish in a white light after demons ripped them apart. Three demons exploded in a flash of blue light as other Navajo angels swung the silver horns. Richard's sword dipped in silver took the head of a gargoyle that covered him in a black liquid; there was no flash of light for the colonel as he thrust his sword in the chest of another, sending it to its death.

Jack directed his sight back to the chamber floor where he saw the Chief's great feathered wings span outward, followed by Andelko's wings that were made of human skin. They both shot upward and began spinning like a whirlwind as sword and tomahawk flashed red and white light with every blow of contact.

Jack fought his way down to where Lina was still motionless at the base of the flat rock that supported the Ark. He put his fingers to her neck; her pulse was silent, which made Jack's heart sink further. The feeling of defeat began to overwhelm him; on his knees, the preacher searched for an answer.

"Lord, have you brought me this far only to lose the earth to such evil?"

Jack looked up for a response but all he saw were more angels being overcome by the large numbers of demons. They were losing fast; Jack stood, and when he did so his foot kicked something. His mind went back to a time when this was how he flushed out bottles of whiskey left by him in a drunken stupor. He looked down expecting to see a bottle laying on its side but instead there laid a ram's horn dropped by a fallen soldier of the Navajo angels. Something or someone told him to blow that trumpet; so he picked it up, took a deep breath and blew as hard and as long as his lungs would allow. The sound could be heard over the peals of thunder and the cracks of lightning from the storm that churned overhead. The gargoyles screeched with pain but there were no angels left to slay them. Blue lightning shot down out of the swirling black clouds and came together between the Cherubs at the golden lid of the Ark of the Covenant and then arched from Cherub to Cherub, shooting six streams of blue lightning upward and reaching out to the tombs that held the slumbering Knights Templar. The entire cave flashed with white light as the ancient warriors came to life from their stone forms; they dropped down from their tombs, one after the other, yielding great swords and shields that bore the Red Cross.

The horn that Jack held burned his hand as it turned to ashes and then to dust and crumbled to the floor. Jack watched with awe as the knights who were the keepers of the Ark systematically moved forward like a wave and with many blows of their blades turned the demons to dust, attacking until every one of them was no more. After they had slain every last soldier from hell they simply vanished like ghosts, leaving the tomb shelves empty for eternity.

Jack looked down to Lina where she lay still; Richard was at the top tier of the steps across the other side of the cave with sword in hand, alone and bloody but seeming no worse for wear. White Owl flew over and landed on the carved stone step next to Richard; his wings retracted and vanished, making his head dress flutter in its breeze as they both stood looking down at Jack and the lifeless Lina. Before Jack could yell out a question it was immediately answered; from the eye of the storm where the four blood moons shone, Andelko descended from the sky riding on the back of the dragon horse and landed on the floor of the arena some twenty feet in front of Jack. The dragon horse had changed and was now a different form of beast, it had ten horns and seven red heads of the dragon held by long necks and Andelko had the numbers 666 burned in his forehead. Jack's eyes were wide, for he could barely believe his eyes. The scriptures of The Book of Revelation went through his mind, but it was not quite right. There were too many discrepancies from what was written. Jack suddenly knew he could defeat this evil, or at the least he would die trying. The preacher's warrior instincts took over and he went into action; he had one pistol with five shots left, for he had not had time to reload. Jack pulled his left handed Colt and began to fire, pulling the hammer down with his thumb and aiming for the heads of the dragon; four out of five of the silver bullets hit their mark, the fifth bullet took one eye from a dragon head, he witnessed it heal over quickly. Four of the beast's necks dropped, leaving three with one blinded on one side; it seemed to throw the dragon beast off balance slightly. Jack cradled his empty pistol and raised his sword; he took the high guard and preparing for a charge by Andelko and his dragon beast.

Colonel Richard intended to fight by Jack's side, but Chief White Owl had halted his descent with one grasp of the man's arm.

"I must stand by my brother's side in his time of need," pleaded Richard, looking down at his arm where the old Indian had ahold of him. He was surprised at the strength that the Chief held.

"This is something that he must do alone, for it is his destiny," The Chief explained.

"I cannot stand by and do nothing," Richard said.

"We can still save the woman, Colonel, but leave the vampire and the beast to the preacher."

White Owl and Richard stealthily went for Lina to remove her from the area of the battle. Her body still lay on the side of the Ark's stone platform on the far side behind where the beast and the vampire and the preacher battled.

Andelko swung his sword from his saddle, several blows to the necks of the dragon cutting the dead weight to the cave floor, and allowing the beast to regain its balance—black blood spewed and dripped from the wounds briefly before healing instantly. Jack launched an attack as the red dragon reared up and out of his reach. He spotted Richard and the chief working their way to secure Lina's body, which gave Jack some hope that she yet might be saved; he flanked Andelko, drawing them away from the Ark and giving his warrior brothers time to flee with the Indian woman that held two souls within her.

Richard and the chief carried Lina away to the outskirts of the battle arena and around the rim to where the horses were kept by the planned exit for leaving the mountain. Jack glanced in their direction as they disappeared behind the stone wall; he then changed his tactics. Jack began a spin with the sword of silver outstretched and moving forward quickly at the dragon; he closed the gap between himself and the beast and after the third spin his blade cut once into the chest of the dragon beast, another quick spin in the opposite direction the sword cut deeper and another spin, it then penetrated even deeper still. A shriek of pain echoed throughout the cave as the red dragon's chest opened wide with a mixture of the flash of the blue light and black blood that ran like a river. Jack was knocked off his feet from the flow of the sticky liquid that smelled of rotting flesh. Andelko flew from the back of the falling beast but managed to land on his feet; Jack rolled out of the way just before he was crushed by the falling beast. The remaining dragon heads bit at the air before crashing to the ground and thrashing to their death. Breathing hard, the preacher crawled on all fours away from the carcass and out of the muddy mess that covered the ground before getting to his feet; he turned and somehow was quick enough to swing his sword and block the blow that would have surely split him in two. Andelko was pushing him backwards in a flurry of blows; Jack recovered enough to stand his ground and battle back as blue and red light flashed brightly throughout the cavern...

White Owl and Richard set Lina gently down on the ground next to where the horses were corralled in front of the exit way.

"There is no heartbeat that can be felt," said Richard with his fingers pressed against the woman's neck.

"Things are not always what they seem," calmly replied White Owl as he pressed both of his palms over the left side of her bosom.

"Yeah, tell me about it, Chief!" said the Colonel.

White Owl turned to look at Richard, "You are sounding more and more like the Preacher as time goes by."

"I will take that as a complement, sir."

White Owl turned his attention back to Lina and closed his eyes. "Back away, Colonel Richard Andersson, I will need some room."

Richard backed away and watched in amazement as the old Indian's wings of feather shot out from his back in an impressive span. A white light glowed all around him as life breathed into the girl, her chest heaved upward and her eyes opened with a look of surprise. "Jack?" escaped her lips.

The preacher was fighting for his life, searching for an edge against the master vampire Andelko Balas; he then heard Lina's voice whisper his name. *She's alive,* he thought. Jack felt his soul come to life and his spirit fill with the eternal light. A rush of strength came over him as he began to overpower Andelko and push him backwards; he saw fear in Andelko's eyes as the red glow diminished, leaving only the bloodshot pupils of a young man with spoiled wealth that had lived once a long time ago. Jack would take Andelko's head, but not as he did before; the preacher slashed his sword down from the high guard position and split the master vampire in half from the point of his head through the body and exiting between the legs, splitting him right down the middle in a flash of white light that shot to the heavens. As the vampire's sword dropped to the ground, the right side of his body fell to the floor, followed by the left side of his torso that teetered on one foot before falling outward to lay in rest. Jack straightened up from his battle stance and watched as the two halves of the master vampire's body turned to dust and vanished from sight.

The cave was suddenly silent and the clouds remained dark but still. Andelko Balas was dead, along with his army of demons. The carcass of the red dragon horse had vanished and Jack felt that the angels of the Navajo nation were finally at peace. Jack set his sights upon the Ark of the Covenant that rested quietly on its pedestal of stone; the gold-laden box seemed to have lost some of its shine.

"Preacher!" cried Lina as she ran up and wrapped her arms around Jack's neck and kissed his cheek several times. Jack embraced her with joy, but he had a hard time taking his eyes off the Ark. Richard approached the preacher and placed his hand on Jack's shoulder and squeezed. "You are a great warrior, my brother, and will be remembered throughout the ages."

Lina gave Jack some room as he raised his arms up and looked around the cave. "I have some doubt brother, for there is not one witness to see and know what happened here."

"We will know, Preacher, and your God knows," Richard replied.

"Our God, brother." Jack turned to White Owl, who stood quietly off to the side.

"I'm gonna open that box, Chief, and see what's inside, I need to see what men have been protecting and dying for over these thousands of years."

White Owl stood without expression and said nothing.

"I'll take that as you're giving me your permission?" Jack questioned as he then made his way over to the Ark and slowly laid his hands upon it. He was expecting to feel something but there was nothing, no energy, no white light, nothing. Richard was now by his side; Jack grabbed ahold of one Cherub and nodded to Richard, who then grabbed the other—they slid the lid off and set it on the ground. A dusty fog lingered as Jack peered inside; he waved his hand to clear the musty air to reveal two stone tablets looking exactly as was described in the scriptures. He did not read ancient Hebrew, but he knew every word that was written upon them. The preacher reached in, intending to pick one tablet up; but when he touched it both tablets turned instantly to dust like ashes of a fire that has turned cold after extinguishing all of its fuel.

"I don't understand." Jack muttered. "It's just gone forever?"

White Owl was suddenly by their side as Jack and Richard stared into the empty box.

"Recall your scripture, Preacher, the Christ died for man's sins to give them eternal life, for man was not capable of following the laws written by God."

"Yes, Chief, the New Testament releases man from living under the curse of the law by the crucifixion, the death and the resurrection of God's only begotten son. We have stopped the Armageddon for now, and put the world back on the path of what has been written."

Richard said with curiosity in his voice, "The tablets have been protected by the Knights Templar for all of these thousands of years and they have now served their purpose."

"Yes, this is right," the Chief acknowledged the Colonel. He then turned back to the preacher. "Matthew, Mark, Luke and John, and Timothy, James, Peter, John and Jude, all prophets and the writers of scripture of the New Testament. There is one other prophet, one book that is lost and you, Preacher, will be the one to discover it and set it at its rightful place after Jude and before Revelation."

Jack stared at the old Indian, trying to figure out exactly what the White Owl was telling him, when suddenly the ground began to shake and the still black clouds began to churn once again.

"I suggest we leave this place at once," the Colonel announced.

Without words they quickly ran for the horses; they were knocked from side to side as the cave floor moved and cracked. Jack led Lina, as they quickly followed White Owl and Richard, who reached the make-shift corral first; the horses were spooked badly and were a handful as they led them up the narrow corridor towards the exit. Lightning flashed and the peals of thunder hurt their ears as it echoed constantly throughout the cavern. They followed a slight luminance of light from the outside as dust and small pieces of rock pummeled their heads. White Owl and Richard were the first to exit the mountain, followed closely by Lina then Jack whose black stallion made it out only by seconds before the tunnel collapsed. The wind was blowing hard as all four mounted, and rode hard to get as far away from the mountain cave as possible. White Owl led them to the same ridge where Andelko and his army once stood. The ground was solid and non-moving and the view was spectacular as they lined up on their horses in silence and watched the Tomb of the Ancients crumble to the ground. The lightning's blue color that they were used to seeing over the past few weeks was now its normal color of white and yellow; it struck from the sky in an attack on the mountain that turned it to dust and leaving what looked like a dried up lake bed. The whirlwind stopped and the clouds split and broke apart and for the first time in over a week, the setting sun shone over the horizon. It was the most beautiful sunset that anyone of them could ever remember witnessing. Jack had the feeling that the days and nights were back on their normal time table.

The night had fallen and they sat around a fire up atop the ridge; after a short prayer of thanks, they ate the last of their meat and beans and unleavened bread that Lina had prepared. The night was bright with clear skies filled with stars and a full moon of great brilliance that hung low and seemed close enough that a man could reach out and touch it. There was a pleasance in the air like they had never felt before; the evil that had surrounded them for months was gone. The animals that roamed the night were out in abundance. The owl swooped down and plucked a mouse from the earth, a split second before a side-winder struck another rodent for its next meal. Jack turned his head to hear a howl off in the distance; the cry was clearly a coyote and not that of a wolf, this proclaimed that the desert had returned to normal.

White Owl sat Indian style, smoking his pipe; his headdress flowed proudly in the light breeze while Lina poured coffee for Richard and then Jack. She joined them with a cup of her own; they all looked upon the chief for some time, waiting patiently for him to speak. Jack smiled and gave a short laugh and shook his head in thought, *just once you'd think the old man would speak out without me having to poke and prod at him.* Jack then asked the question they were all thinking.

"Andelko Balas is dead for good this time, Chief, I am sure of it, but what do we do now?"

"The evil that was the master vampire is dead, this is true," said Chief White Owl of the Navajo, "the fallen-one who reigns in hell has already begun his plans for his next attack on the souls of man."

Jack, Lina and Richard all looked at one another and then back to White Owl. Jack questioned further.

"The evil-one's plans to speed up and change the writings of the book of Revelation has failed—you said there was one more book of lost writings of the bible to be found, is this right?

"Not lost preacher," replied the chief, "un-written."

"Un-written?" said Richard with some confusion. "The book of God is the oldest script on this world; it has always been thought to be complete."

"The Devil's tricks have put much time between the miracle that is the Christ and end times," the chief paused for a moment and took a deep draw on his pipe. "Man has been given a third chance to have eternal life, Adam and Eve being the first and Jesus of Nazareth being the second."

"So what your sayin', Chief, is that we need to find the lost prophet?" Jack asked.

"Lost? said White Owl as he searched deep into Jack's eyes with his own. "Not lost, found; you are the prophet, Jack."

Jack's mouth dropped slightly and then he sprung to his feet. "What in the heck are you talkin' about, Chief?"

White Owl looked to Lina; she stood and faced Jack. "I am with child."

Jack's mouth slammed shut and he instantly looked at his brother Richard, who shook his head just slightly as he then stood. Jack was confused, angry and jealous all at the same time, he turned back to Lina and grabbed her shoulders a little harder than he had meant too. "But we have not laid down together in that way!"

"I have not lain with any man, for I am a virgin."

Jack was in shock from what he had just heard, and Richard had to grab ahold to steady him before he fell; they all sat back down on the ground and Chief White Owl stood and spread his wings before them—he spoke to them for the last time. "And she shall bring forth a second son, and thou shalt call his name Constantine; for he shall save his people from their sins."

With a sweep of his hand, the Archangel named Gabriel, known to the Preacher as Chief White Owl, sent the three into a deep sleep as he vanished in a bright white light that reached the heavens until he was gone.

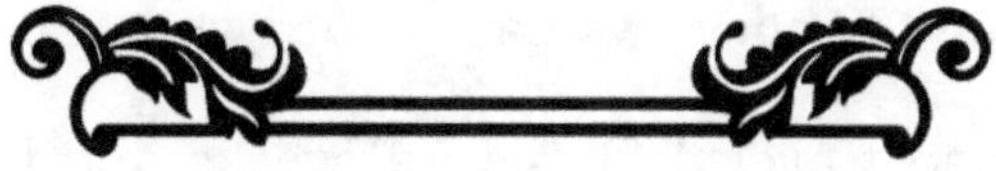

CHAPTER SEVENTEEN

When the sun rose, the preacher Jack Denton Anderson, Lina, who was the last of her Apache clan, and Colonel Richard Andersson a soldier of Croatian decent, awoke refreshed and with a pleasant heart. The sun was shining and the weather was at a degree of perfection. They rose to their feet and gazed across the extinguished fire to see that Chief White Owl of the Navajo had vanished along with his horse. Jack put his hand on mother Lina's slight belly mound and smiled with glee. She smiled back at him and placed her palm on his beard stubble that had grown on his face. Jack smiled and nodded toward his brother Richard, who also seemed to have aged. Lina had the appearance of a woman who was three months pregnant, but her aging was barely noticeable, as her age could not be more than twenty years. The second son of God would be named Constantine; the second Messiah whose name meant, 'Steadfast, reliable, faithful and true to the end'. Constantine would be the King warrior of all the people.

"Where might our travels lead us, Preacher?" Richard asked as they prepared the horses for travel.

"Scripture tells me east, a place called Bethlehem, my brother."

"Israel?"

"Not quite that far to the east; Bethlehem, Texas. But first we must maneuver this canyon and reach a town I know of—we need a new horse for mother Lina, a black, and I believe we have outgrown our clothes."

They had traveled for several weeks and had found the town with the clothing store next to a saloon that Jack knew well from his days without faith. He remembered spotting the all-black garb of the evangelist in the window long ago and wondered if he would one day earn the right to wear it. He and Richard both wore the long black cloaks that concealed their Colt revolvers, but only Jack wore the white cloth around his neck. The wide, straight brim black hats complemented the hilts of the swords that protruded at their backs. Lina now wore a long black dress made from the same cloth as her husband and his brother that blended in well with her new black Shetland pony. The dress was loose enough to conceal her pregnancy and over her shoulder hung a set of Colt Dragoon revolvers. They paid the merchant with one piece of gold, a piece of a wing of a Cherub, removed from the rubble that was once perched on top of an ancient golden box.

Every night under the stars the prophet Jack would write down the day's events while Brother Richard and the virgin mother Lina would melt silver bullets over the fire to fight the evil that was now following them across the open desert.

~ * ~

The End of the Beginning

May the grace of our Lord Jesus Christ be with us all! Amen.

About the Author

Bret Lee Hart, a second generation Floridian, has spent the last twenty-five years in Marine construction; he is married and the father of two. His mother's maiden name is Emerson, as in Ralph Waldo, and on his father's side, Edgar Allen Poe can be found hanging on the family tree. With this bloodline of writers, and being named after Bret Harte from his western short stories, it was inevitable his imagination would find its way into print.

The *Half-Breed Gunslinger, Hunter James Dolin (Book II), Montgomery's Revenge (Book III), Wanted*

Dead (Book IV), and Wars End (Book V) are the five books in this "cracker Western" series, as Bret calls them, and are available at major online book retailers.

The Fangslinger and the Preacher, Preacher Jack and the Fangslinger (Book II) are also available with many other adventures soon to be unleashed from this exciting storyteller's mind in various genres, including Fantasy and the Paranormal.

Follow Bret Lee Hart on Facebook:
https://facebook.com/bretleehart

OTHER WORKS AVAILABLE FROM
BRET LEE HART

✳ ✳ ✳ ✳ ✳

*~ A Paranormal Western based on the
age-old battle of good versus evil ~*

Master Andelko Balas is the leader of a bored, and therefore troublesome, vampire coven in Romania in the 1880s. Colonel Richard Andersson brings relief to the boredom by discovering tales of the American West and setting the coven on an exciting, but bloody, journey to a new land.

Jack Denton, reformed gunfighter, former preacher, now a drunkard, has visions of a great evil coming to Arizona as he wanders in the desert. Then he meets an Indian Chief and is given a silver sword, a special cross, and a mission. Jack is led to Black Mountain

Mesa where an unusual storm is brewing and he has to face the greatest battle of his life.

Is this the last battle for the world as he knows it? Will his renewed faith and special weapons be enough to defeat such evil?

Brief Excerpt:
Black Mesa Mountain, Arizona, 1885
He went by the name Preacher Jack, given to him by his small congregation in New Mexico. He had buried the name Anderson in the past, going by the name Jack Denton in fear of being discovered by the law, or the lawless. It was a simple life he now led, and a good life for Preacher Jack, until God's plan for him continued forward. When his wife and daughter died from disease that swept through the small Mexican village, Jack lost his faith in God and left New Mexico, wandering aimlessly, not caring if he lived or died. Forty-year-old Jack Denton, a fallen preacher, was now a faithless drunkard living off whiskey – his only thoughts were of drinking himself to death.

Forty days and forty nights into his journey of despair, Jack found refuge in an abandoned mining shack to get some rest. A vision appeared to him as he slept, the drunken haze in which he slumbered left him, allowing the vivid images of his dream to come forth...

Fear overwhelmed him as something that Jack could only describe as a demon straight from hell swooped down on top of him, baring bloody fangs to devour his flesh.

Jack Denton awoke with a scream from the dirt floor of the mining shack.

* * * * *

~ The Paranormal Western sequel to
"The Fangslinger and the Preacher" ~

Preacher Jack and his comrade Richard, a centuries-old Romanian soldier, thought their battle against evil was won after their climactic battle with the master vampire Andelko Balas at the top of Black Mountain Mesa. But Richard's former master was not vanquished permanently; the Fallen One has raised him up, and now Balas has an undead army at his command. The Preacher and the Fangslinger, aided by the mystical Indian White Owl and his followers, are now all that stands in the way of the vampire master's plan to empower his dark lord and unleash hell on earth.

Will the Preacher's faith be strong enough to sustain them?

Brief Excerpt:

On his return to camp, Jack was surprised to see that Richard had pulled himself up and was now leaning against a flat rock formation alongside the campsite that partially blocked the dry desert wind. As Jack got closer he could see that the color in Richard's face was much better. Jack then realized that the colonel had positioned himself in a shady spot to avoid the rays of the morning light. This concerned the Preacher, for this was something a man with the blood of a vampire might do.

"Does the sun bother you?" Jack asked.

"Slightly, yes," answered Richard, "may I bother you for some additional water?"

Jack fetched the canteen and went to one knee as he handed it over, but this time Jack did so at a greater distance.

Richard took several small sips, and then the two men stared at one another for a moment.

"You do not trust me so?"

"Ain't sure just yet," answered Jack, "you did save my life on that mountain, and the rumor is that we are kin, but the simple fact that you're hidin' from the sun does got me wonderin'."

✳ ✳ ✳ ✳ ✳

~ A Western action adventure, the first in
"The Half-Breed Gunslinger" *series ~*

In 1860 there was more open range cattle in Florida than in Texas and all the other states combined. It took a special breed of man to live there, and an even harder man to survive. Hunter James Dolin, half white and half Indian, was such a man. He was a gambler by trade and a gunslinger of necessity and attracted trouble wherever he traveled. But with his two Colt Walkers and bowie knife, he could handle almost anything.

Brief excerpt:

About ninety miles back and a few days earlier, in the crackerjack Saloon along the Withlacoochee River, Dolin's ace-high straight flush had beat one of the three outlaws' full house. He won fair and square – two ounces of gold and a just 'broke in' Henry rifle. These days that was more than reason enough to kill a man.

Hunter had felt the itch in his craw that warned him he'd out-stayed his welcome, and knew it was high time for him to leave this place. Without taking his eyes off the men at the poker table, Hunter had gathered up his winnings, while he spoke, "Thank you, Gentlemen. It's been a pleasure."

The man at the table to Hunter's left, the one who just lost his Henry rifle, had stood and replied angrily, "Do you think we're just gonna let you walk on out of here, half-breed?"

* * * * *

Spurred by revenge...
Gunfights and gold...
One man against the odds...

Hunter James Dolin survived the revenge war of Myakka City, Florida, by killing the men who raised their guns against him and his loved ones – all but one.

The Governor directed the Army to investigate, forcing the Half-Breed Gunslinger to seek refuge deep in the swamps of the Everglades.

Hunter James Dolin was content to live the rest of his life in solitude – 'til he was sought out and told of the whereabouts of the one that got away.

This would spark a new battle of revenge, overshadowed by the Civil War, but not soon forgotten by the people who inhabit the Florida swamplands.

Brief excerpt:

Scooter was swinging like a pendulum as very large Gators came up out of the water and snapped at the chicken, just out of reach of the man's head. Scooter was screaming again, as Hunter backed Zeke up a bit, putting his face and head closer to the teeth-laden jaws of the twelve-foot reptiles. The largest of the Gators stretched his neck up and snapped two pieces of chicken hanging down less than a foot from Scooter Johnson's head.

"PULL ME UP!!!! PULL ME UP!!!!" shrieked the dangling man. "I'm not the last – Montgomery's alive! *HE'S ALIVE, PLEASE!!!"*

Hunter urged the Appaloosa forward so the rope hanging over the branch moved with him, pulling Scooter up and out of reach of the Gator's bite.

"What do you mean, *he's alive?*" yelled Hunter. "I blowed him up in his own hotel."

✳ ✳ ✳ ✳ ✳

~ A Western action adventure, the third in "The Half-Breed Gunslinger" series, set in Florida. Author Bret Lee Hart reminds us his state was once as wild as the West – and just as deadly. ~

Duke Montgomery is an Indian fighter – a hard-as-nails killer, plain and simple – who doesn't think twice about ambushing a man or killing him face-to-face. When he learns his brother Richard is dead, killed by the Half-Breed Gunslinger, Duke goes on the hunt.

To avoid trouble after his dealings with Richard Montgomery, Hunter James Dolin and the woman, Helen, travel deep into the Everglades to live in peace for a while. But, as is the way of the world, trouble soon comes looking for them.

How many will die as Montgomery seeks the Half-Breed Gunslinger to get revenge? And what surprises are in store for Hunter James Dolin?

Brief Excerpt:
"Where you headed, mister?" asked Billy.

"Myakka City is my first stop," replied Duke.

"Where's that at, Billy?" whispered Junior, leaning toward Billy.

"Not sure," said Billy, "Where's that city at, Mister? Maybe we could tag along with yah?"

There it was; Duke had just recruited these two easily with his larger mind. He grabbed the whiskey bottle by its neck, and with the other hand chugged the last of his beer then slammed the glass mug on the counter. "We leave tomorrow mornin' at sunup, meet me at the hotel. You will be paid if you do your jobs and don't git yourself killed." Duke turned and headed for the door, taking his whiskey bottle with him.

"What might our jobs be?" said Billy to his back.

The shirtless, scarred, muscle man stopped and turned after two steps. "We're going to Florida to kill a stinkin' half-breed."

Billy and Junior looked at one another and grinned with confidence that the job would be easy enough.

"What do your friends call you, Mister?" Junior asked.

"I don't have any friends, but you will call me Sir." Duke turned and walked out, leaving the saloon doors swinging behind him.

✳ ✳ ✳ ✳ ✳

*~ A Western action adventure, the forth in
"The Half-Breed Gunslinger" series, set in Florida.*

While *The Half-Breed Gunslinger* fights for his life against infection from a gunshot wound, there are wanted posters being printed with his name and likeness. A $5,000 bounty on the head of Hunter James Dolin is more than enough money to attract men to the swamps of south Florida. The ending of the Civil War turns soldiers into bounty hunters as the North feels the need to cleanse the South, and men find ways to make a living.

The gunslinger's woman carries his child; Helen will need help from their close friends as her pregnancy progresses. Jebidiah and Walt will protect Helen at all costs with their experience and grit. Bodie and Bird, with their own skills, will be by their side in whatever comes their way. To their surprise, unexpected rivals come after the newly named Dolin Family.

Brief excerpt:
"What's goin' on, Hunter? Talk to me."

"Bounty hunter keeping track of our whereabouts." Helen's hand went to the butt of her gun. "Easy, woman; he's gone for now, but he will be back and with friends."

"What will we do?" she asked calmly.

"We can't stay here, it's too open. We could hold them off inside the cabin but for only so long; eventually they would burn us out. Myakka City is where our friends are; they will increase our numbers."

"Then we'll git little James, Alameda and Mocha and go to town at once."

"It ain't safe for the boy or you. I think maybe you should take little James and go with Alameda to the Seminole tribe lands..." Before he could finish, Helen was on her feet and shaking her head.

"I will not stay with that Sam Jones; Alameda can take little James and Mocha out there but I will go where you go." She turned and began walking up the bank to the cabin. "We best git packin'."

Hunter knew Helen meant to stand firm on her decision and there was nothing he could say to change her mind once she had made it. The boy would be safest with the tribe and Helen's skill with the gun would be handy. She had been battle tested and had killed without prejudice. She would be more dangerous now that she was a mother, like a mamma bear protecting her cub.

* * * * *

~ *A Western action adventure, the fifth in
"The Half-Breed Gunslinger" series, set in Florida.*

The three year Montgomery/ Dolin War was over, and not one family member named Montgomery was left alive. Hunter James Dolin had killed Richard Montgomery, his brother Duke Montgomery and their sister Jane Montgomery. The next man in line named Little Owl, for Chief of the Snake Clan of the Miccosukee, of the Seminole Indian Tribe was killed by the hand of the Half-Breed Gunslinger. Little Owl and his loyal braves were no more.

Myakka City and the James family had survived the last battle and Helen and little James were found alive at the waters' edge. Their current enemies were dead but Hunter was concerned about the wanted posters. There was no way to know how many had been printed and how far they had spread? The authors of the prints were dead but it would take time for this to be known and then believed. Five thousand dollars was a world of money and there would be men coming to kill the Half-breed Gunslinger and seeking their fortune.

Brief excerpt:
"The knife," said Hooker.

Hunter reached back and pulled the bowie from the sheath that was clipped to his pants at his back. Daryl took that too, with the same grin, only bigger.

"You take good care of that, Daryl; I will be needin' that back."

The stare of the gunslinger's steel blue eyes froze Daryl for a moment. His smile faded and then came back, but only a little.

"Oh, you won't need this no more, half-breed, not where you goin'."

"Daryl! I'm only gonna tell yah one more time to shut the hell up," the Captain warned. "Jimbo, tie his hands in the front; he's got to ride."

The big mouth drover picked up Hunter's pistol belt from the floor as Jimbo escorted the gunslinger outside. Zeke was there, and Hunter was placed on his back by two of the men.

"Where we headed, Captain?" Hunter asked.

"Daryl and Jimbo here will take you to Fort Foster and we'll let the army decide your fate."

"What of my family, Captain?" Hunter asked.

"When they are ready for travel I will personally escort them wherever they would like to go, unharmed. I give you my word as a lawman and a gentleman."

"You do as you say, Captain, and I will allow you to live. I give you my word, but your men here, a pass will not be givin'."

Jimbo glared at Hunter and Daryl laughed out loud.

"Let's go, tough guy," Jimbo replied.

"You try anythin', half-breed, and I'll kill yah with your own guns," Daryl said while resting his hand on Hunter's 44s that he now wore on his hip.

Hunter was glad to see his bowie knife tucked in the man's belt for he would need it as well on his return.